THE DEVIL'S
HOST MC

The Complete Series

SHARI SLADE

Christine,

You are a total
Rockstar.
Enjoy the ride
Shari
Slade

Cover design by Book Beautiful
Print formatting by Romanced by the Cover

Contents

When a big scary biker shows up at Jimmy's Diner fifteen minutes before the end of my shift—covered in tattoos and looking at me like I'm on the menu—I should flip the open sign to closed.

But I don't.

I'm too used to doing what I've been told. Too used to working and struggling and surviving to do anything different. A closed sign wouldn't stop him anyway. He's here to collect a debt. And I'm the only one left to pay.

Praise for The Devil's Host MC

"Intense, dangerous, and perfectly dirty! Ride Me Hard will leave you breathless."

> – *New York Times* Bestselling author
> Skye Warren

"So damn hawt!"

> – Bookaholic Babe

"RIDE ME HARD has a panty-melting mix of sex, sass and sin. It hooked me hard."

> – Heidi Joy Tretheway author
> of *Tattoo Thief*

"This was an addictive start to a new series that I definitely want to read more of."

> – The Scarf Princess

"From the first word to the last my stomach was clenched tight in a 'god what on earth is going to happen next' tension."

> – Gemma Reads Too Much

Dedication

For Lizard, who listens

RIDE ME HARD

PART 1 OF 4

ONE

Twelve hours into what should be an eight-hour shift and my new uniform still feels foreign on my body. Scratchy and wrong. Unpleasantly damp. Yesterday I'd worn jeans and a Jimmy's Diner T-shirt. Tonight, I'm packed into a polyester dress that looks like it came from a catalog full of naughty Halloween costumes—1950s Pinup or Sexy Soda Jerk.

I tug at the powder-blue skirt barely covering my ass and adjust the ruffled apron. Who thought white aprons were a good idea in a restaurant full of ketchup, jam and gravy? Jimmy Jr. *The idiot.*

I wince.

Hot coals have replaced the muscles in the small of my back; that's the only explanation for the searing pain that radiates with every wobbly step I take. My new management-issued shoes are as ridiculous and nonfunctional as the dress, strappy black Mary Janes with pointy toes, pointier heels, and some kind of no-skid treatment on the soles. Thank God for small favors.

The whole tacky getup cost eighty bucks. Cheap, but still too rich for my blood. The cherry on top of one very shitty sundae. At least they'd take it out of my check in installments, because I'd barely made a quarter of that tonight, proving once and for all that waitresses are invisible no matter what they're wearing. Jimmy's Diner is invisible too, now that the new bypass is finished and the truckers can barrel past town doing eighty miles per hour.

The locals coming in for early bird specials aren't going to cut it, and no sexy gimmick will replace the volume of being on a high-traffic truck route. Short of throwing up a roadblock and diverting traffic, Jimmy is fucked.

I dip my hand into my apron pocket and stroke the tiny wad of singles, reassuring myself it's still there. Five to shove in the coffee can I keep under the sink and then...not even enough to fill a gas tank, let alone make a dent in the weekly rent my landlord is salivating over. He's already looking for any excuse to eject me from the little garage apartment his new wife wants to use for a craft studio.

I'm pretty fucked too.

It's not like I'm working here by choice. If this job bottoms out...I can't even think about that particular dead end. Instead I focus on the present...fifteen-minute increments. I can survive anything for fifteen minutes. I know that from experience.

Fifteen more minutes without a customer and I can lock the doors, kick off these torture devices, and finish the last of my side work.

I pull out the tiny funnels and the big buckets of salt and pepper to do the most boring sand art ever. That's my life. Boring, painful, and thanks to the bypass and circumstance, cut off from the rest of the world.

I can hear my cousin Harry singing in the kitchen, and I know he's mopping up. He always sings while he mops. Humming along with him at the end of a shift makes me feel like a part of something. Not a family exactly, but something.

I wouldn't have this job if it weren't for him. Not that he'd done much other than tell Jimmy I needed work. Sometimes *not much* is all it takes to make a difference.

Fifteen more minutes and he'll haul the trash out to the dumpster and lock the back door behind him. If I time it right, we can leave together. I poke my head through the window where he sets the orders as they're finished. "Can you give me a ride home tonight?"

"I don't know, Star. I've got stops to make." He twitches and wipes sweat from his neck with a bandanna before swishing dirty water over the floor again. Like I don't know about his stops late at night? Probably to see the same people that sometimes pop into the diner, also twitching and sweating. Looking for pills or meth. I'm not sure. I don't even really care as long as I don't have to walk home alone in the dark.

"But—" Harry spins around with the mop like he's twirling a lover and bumps the prep table. Three beer bottles crash to the floor, and I notice a fourth is clutched in his hand along with the mop handle. I decide not to argue with his weak excuse or to remind him we're family—no matter how distant. It's not worth it.

"That's okay, Harry. I can walk just fine."

Sure I can. It's only fifteen minutes to get home. I hobble back to my shakers.

A bark of laughter, deep and rough, startles me from behind, and my first thought is *son of a bitch* because if that's a new customer wanting dinner, all my fifteen-minute plans have turned into an hour at least.

"Looks like you've got a little hitch in your giddyup, sweetheart. Why don't you bring me a menu and come sit on my lap?"

I whirl around to tell him right where he can put a damn menu, and my breath catches.

I can't process all of him at once. He's that big. He is scruff and muscle and a white T-shirt tucked into dusty jeans. He looks weathered and road weary, like most of Jimmy's clientele, but...more. Everything about him is intense. His knife-blade cheekbones. His heavy brows.

His blue eyes flash icy heat, and some animal instinct tells me this man isn't looking for sass, that if he finds it, he might do something about it, something I won't like at all.

He's made himself comfortable in the booth with his leather jacket tossed on the opposite side along with a sleek black helmet. I'm pretty sure there's a motorcycle parked out front now to match his accessories. If only I'd heard the rev of an engine and the spray of gravel, but I was too busy humming and watching the clock. A warning would've been nice. I might have locked the door a few minutes early, even if it did mean Jimmy would dock my pay.

No. I wouldn't have locked a customer out. But I'd have braced myself better.

His hands are massive and flat on the tabletop. Tattoos crisscross his blunt knuckles, the ink broken by spidery scars. It takes my brain precious seconds to decipher the blue-black loops and whirls as letters.

It's like he's put them there for inspection. But not the "clean enough for supper, ma'am?" kind of inspection, the "how much damage do you think these can do?" kind.

A lot of damage. That's the answer. A lot. Those are knuckles that have been through walls and windows. Flesh and bone.

I want to say we're closed, but Jimmy'd can my ass for turning away a paying customer. I want to run back to the kitchen and get Harry to tell him to take his business elsewhere, but Harry isn't any match for this man. And I'm frozen in place anyway. I can't peel my eyes away from his hands.

I stare harder, and it hits me that the letters over his knuckles form words.

Lost. Soul.

Some fear inside me eases, because that's almost romantic. Lost souls and lone wolves. Desperadoes. If he were really terrible, he wouldn't have to advertise. The truly dangerous men blend in.

"Not much of a talker, are you?" he says.

I try for caustic, but the words slip out as half whispers. "Not when I don't have anything to say."

He laughs again, only softer this time. More smug. "I can respect that."

Him respecting anything about me seems like the most ridiculous thing yet. Even sillier than me standing here for long minutes without taking his order. My gaze drifts up his colorful forearms, across his chest, and over the hard pecs I can make out through thin cotton. His neck, corded with muscle and more ink, flexes under my scrutiny.

Everything about him is hard, except for his mouth.

His lips look soft. And pinker than they should be. A sensual mouth, curled into a smile that says *I know everything you're thinking, and yeah you're exactly right*. A smile that says *test me, please*. A smile that says *I'm hungry and you look like cake*.

Fuck me. I want to be cake.

He is every bad decision I've ever made all rolled up into one terrifying package. I blow out a shaky breath. *Focus on the job. Focus on the next fifteen minutes*. "I'm Star, and I'll be your server tonight. Would you like to hear the specials?"

I've offered that same greeting to hundreds of customers. Maybe thousands. Why does it sound exactly like *eat me* when I say it to him?

"That wasn't so bad, was it? Unfortunately for both of us, this stop is business, not pleasure. Now be a good girl and go tell that tweaker in the kitchen I'm here for Dev's money."

Shit. I turn toward the kitchen and barely register the bolt of fire zinging up the back of my heel and into my calf. Before I can take a single step, I hear the unmistakable *thunk* of the back door slamming shut.

Harry has left the building.

A hand snaps around my wrist, shocking the breath out of me and forcing me to turn around.

"I-I'm sure he's just taking out the trash. He'll be right back," I stammer.

"He better be, for your sake."

TWO

The bells on the front door jingle. The big scary biker releases my wrist and slips back into his booth seat. Smooth as silk. Just another customer. Nothing to see here. He nails me to the floor, though, with his eyes and a single whispered word. "Don't."

Don't what? Don't run? Don't scream? Don't...try anything? I've seen this movie. I know what happens, especially in these shoes. Me flat on my face in the parking lot, him looming over me. I shiver.

I just need to find a way to give him what he wants and get him the fuck out of here. I can do this. I squeeze my eyes shut and say a silent prayer that whoever just walked in the door isn't a friend of his. Or a little old lady with a heart condition. Or Harry.

I know for sure it won't be Harry. Goddamn cowardly idiot.

An oily voice crawls over my skin. "Everything okay in here, Star?"

Fuuuuck. If this situation is a brush fire, that voice and the body it's attached to are gasoline.

"Good evening, Officer Wade."

Officer. Officer. Officer. I mentally telegraph that to the biker glowering in the booth beside me. *Don't.*

It echoes in my mind. It echoes in his too, because I watch him slowly curl his fingers around the handle of the steak knife on the table. Is that a threat for me? Or Officer Wade?

Officer Wade helps himself to a slice of pie from the dessert case next to the counter, struts over to his regular booth, and slides into its vinyl embrace. "So formal. I'm not even in uniform."

"That's a shame." And I mean that deeply. If he had his uniform on, he'd have handcuffs and a gun strapped to his belt. He'd have a patrol car out front instead of the little sedan with worn leather seats that smell like french fries. If he had his uniform on, he'd be here in a professional capacity and not trying to get me into the back of his car again for recreational purposes. "We close in ten minutes."

"I know. I came to give you a ride home."

The way he says *ride* makes my stomach twist, and I have to force myself to swallow the *no, thank you* that's become automatic.

Shit. I should be relieved, but the last ride home was all unfortunate hands and his unpleasant mouth slimy on my neck.

And I've been putting him off for weeks. I try to be nice, but it only makes him more aggressive.

I don't know what's worse, the biker clutching a dull knife and vibrating with hostility or the up-standing member of the community who thinks his badge gives him permission to take whatever he wants.

The biker stands, leaving the cutlery on the table, and pulls a worn wallet from the back pocket of his jeans. He drops a wrinkled ten and grabs his gear.

My heart drops, and I have my answer. Officer Wade is worse.

"My compliments to the chef." He hands me the menu. "I can't wait to try the meatloaf."

Tomorrow's special. Message received. He'll be back.

That's fine. I don't work tomorrow anyway.

The door closes behind him, and it's like all the air rushes back into the dining room. Officer Wade barely seems to register the near miss other than to blink at the exit. He just eats his pie. "You about done here?"

Screw the side work. And Jimmy. And dumbass Harry. I don't have any choice but to take Officer Wade up on his offer and hope he can be decent. Maybe he will. Maybe he'll surprise me. I can't exactly walk off into the night with him standing in the parking lot watching. I weigh my options. "Yeah, just let me grab my purse and lock up."

The back door locks by itself, so I flip the kitchen lights without wandering in farther and grab my bag from the cabinet under the register. Jimmy will be pissed if I don't take the cash back to the office safe, but we barely did a hundred dollars in sales since the last cash drop. It hardly seems worth it.

I hold the front door open for Officer Wade, punch in the alarm code, and hurry out before I accidentally set it off.

"Come on, Star. I want to make last call at the Drop before I take you home."

"I'm really tired, Wade. Too tired to drink. I appreciate the escort, though; we had some tough customers tonight."

I fumble with my keys, trying to find the one that fits the sticky exterior lock. How long do I have before the alarm trips? Two minutes? One?

"Like that big bastard in your section when I came in? Glad I was here to serve and protect."

Should I say something? That the *big bastard* threatened me? That he threatened Harry because...something to do with drugs? No. I'm not a narc. And what good would it do anyway? The big bastard is gone. And I'm alone. With Wade. The key slides home with a click.

Who's going to protect me from him?

A clammy hand lands on my thigh and inches up. Wade's touch is worse than cobwebs across my face in a dark basement. I jerk away, but he pins me against the door.

"Please don't, Wade. I'm sorry. I'm just not interested in you that way."

"Star—"

"Hey, asshole." The biker's voice tears across the parking lot. "She fucking said don't."

Wade grunts and then...he's gone. His hand isn't on my leg. His chest isn't heating my back. There's nothing but air behind me.

I can't bring myself to look at what's happening. Because I know. There's more grunting and shouting. The thumps of knuckles against soft flesh. The sick crack of what can only be bone on pavement.

25

Oh God. I have to look. I wobble on my heels and turn to find Wade facedown on the ground, the biker looming over him. His heavy boot resting on the back of Wade's head.

He came back.

For one second I'm so fucking grateful to have Wade's hands off me, however that had to happen. For one second I only care about myself.

"Thank you," I breathe.

"Don't thank me. I was making plans for your ass, and he was getting his fingerprints all over it."

THREE

Wade is out cold; at least I hope that's all he is. I drop to my knees and use two fingers to find a pulse, the way Mrs. Zambroski taught us in eighth grade biology. The thumb side of the wrist. Two fingers. *Don't press too hard.* I take a shuddering breath and hold it.

If he's dead, is it my fault? My throat tightens, and tears prickle up to the surface. Not for Wade. For myself, for this fucked-up situation.

Wade's skin is warmer than I expect, and for one horrible second all I can feel is the thundering of my own heart.

"I didn't kill him." The biker's words rumble over me, but I don't look up. My eyes are locked on the scuffed toe of his massive boot, still resting on the back of Wade's head. Casually.

When I finally find my voice, it's flat—if a little strangled. "You could have."

It's not a question. It's an observation. This is a man who can kill another man. Easy, casual violence. I know that in my bones. Not because he's covered in tattoos and leather, but because he's standing here like he spends all his days using the heads of his enemies for footrests. Maybe he does.

Loose gravel bites into my shins, but I hold still as a steady pulse beats against the pads of my fingers. Thank God. A hot rush of relief courses through me. And then the tears do fall. Fat, salty drops slip over my cheeks and down my chin.

"Yeah, I could have. Could still."

"Because he—he touched me?"

"Oh no, sweetheart. Don't get romantic ideas." He leans down and grabs my chin between his thumb and forefinger, forcing me to look up into his cold eyes. "Because I feel like it."

My heart pounds against my ribs again, frantic and desperate. What else does he feel like doing? "Did you miss the part where he's a cop?"

Because reminding him he's assaulted an officer of the law and has nothing left to lose is a brilliant idea. I gulp at my own stupidity.

"No. But if he's clean, I'm a fucking choir boy. I'm sure he won't want to answer any uncomfortable questions about tonight."

He's got a point, but my stomach twists at the possible blowback. Wade and Jimmy are friends. One word from Wade and Jimmy will eighty-six my job faster than yesterday's special. I scramble for an escape. *We were attacked on the way to the parking lot. A stranger. He probably thought I had the night's deposit in my purse.* It's not far from the truth. It could work. And Wade would seem like a hero. He probably wouldn't argue the details. "I need to call him an ambulance. If I tell you where you might find Harry, will you leave? Please. I won't tell the police anything about you. I promise."

My voice breaks. *I promise?* God, could I be more pathetic?

He tips my chin up farther until it's uncomfortable to hold the position. I wince and resist the urge to pull free. I need him to trust me. Worse, I want him to like me. As much as he tells me not to thank him, not to get romantic ideas…I wonder.

He smirks. "So, he gets to be a hero?"

And there it is again. Does *he* want to be the hero? That wounded smirk is a sliver of hope, that maybe this big bad man likes being good sometimes. Wants it, like something forbidden and sweet. Like cake. Like me. "What? No. I just…I'm trying to help us both out here. We can both get what we want, can't we?"

"I think so." His smirk curls into a genuine smile, one that raises the hair on the back of my neck.

Regret flickers in my belly. I remember that my security comes with a price. "Are you going to hurt Harry?"

"Not if he has Dev's money. But judging by the way he ran off tonight, that might be an issue. If you're worried about him, I might let you plead for his life. You're pretty on your knees. We could do *this* again."

My cheeks heat with arousal and shame as I realize how I must look; face streaked with tears, skirt rucked up almost to my hips, lips inches from his crotch.

Wade's unconscious body between us. Shit. I need to get him out of here before Wade wakes up and my terrible plan falls apart.

"But I won't be—" And then it hits me. He's going to take me with him, and I'm not one-hundred percent sure I don't want to go.

His grip on my chin eases into a caress, and I shiver. His touch is almost tender, swiping away my tears with his thumb. "There's a smart girl. But I'm not a complete monster. I'll bring you back here in a few days, sooner if Harry has the money. You'll only be a little worse for wear, unless you like it rough."

Do I? My lips twitch to say no, to protest, but my body has other ideas.

I shouldn't trust him. I should scream and run and break my ankle trying to get away. Instead I turn my face into his palm like a kitten looking to be petted.

I was worried about him having nothing to lose, but really I'm the one with nothing to lose. Dead-end job, dead-end apartment, dead-end family...I might as well climb on the back of his bike and see where he takes me.

FOUR

In my skirt and heels, I'm not exactly sure how to climb onto the back of his bike. Not without flashing my panties or possibly knocking into something I'm not supposed to touch.

I'm not *supposed* to touch any of this. Not the bike. Not him. I don't even know his name.

Not that it matters. We aren't going to be friends. He isn't going to ask about my day and rub my feet. He's going to… I shake my head against the filthy thoughts shimmering just beneath the surface. Me with my legs spread, him tearing down my…

I take a step toward the bike and hesitate. It's more like a mountain than a bike anyway. A sleek metal mountain, with chrome peaks and flat black valleys.

"What do I— How do I—"

And then he's behind me, arms like tree trunks at my back and under my ass. I am falling and flying and so warm in his embrace as he lifts me up. Bereft when he plants me on the leather seat instead of bending me over it.

"What's your name? Should I even ask that? I shouldn't."

He laughs, skimming his fingers down my leg, catching on my nylons, trailing sparks in the wake of his touch. He plucks at the thin material and opens up a run in my dime-store hose.

"Noah."

It's like a match strike. The sound of the rip, the drag of his calluses over my bare skin. Jagged and sharp and so damn hot. I reach behind me and wrap my hands around the metal bar that seems to exist for just such a purpose. So I can have something to hold on to while he makes me explode by wriggling his rough little finger against a patch of skin just above my knee.

The bastard.

He keeps his head down, and I pretend he doesn't know what he's doing to me, what I'm feeling as he grips my ankle and plants my foot on a little spoke. His hot breath puffs against my outer thigh. Oh, he knows. "You put your feet here."

I find a matching spoke on the left side and center myself on the seat. He studies me for a moment, his careful gaze more efficient than a stroke. It sends a rush of blood to my cheeks and my nipples and lower, making me pink and full. Exposed. I duck my chin, trying to hide the worst of my blush.

He grabs the helmet and lifts it toward me. Oh God, he's going to put the big heavy thing over my head and I'm not going to be able to see or hear anything. Fear slithers in my belly and up into my throat. I forget all about hiding my blush. Hiding anything. I cry out. "Wait— No—"

"Shhh…" He smooths my hair back with one hand and cups my cheek. "I'm making plans for your face too, sweetheart, and they don't include seeing it smashed on the highway."

So he's going to take care of me. At least for now.

He catches my lower lip with his thumb and tugs it down just a little. Not enough to expose my teeth, but enough to let me know his plans for my face include my mouth. I know this dance. On some terrible reflex my tongue darts out, and I taste the mineral salt of him. Copper and stone.

Electric. He feels it too; I know it. Like licking a battery.

He sucks in a breath, and I bow toward him as if he's drawing me in for air. Sucking me down, because he is. With his touch and his grunts and the way he looks at me. He skims down my neck, over my shoulders and my arms, until he's crowding me completely. Almost hugging me. He grips my wrist and presses his face to my ear. A sharp pleasure-pain pierces my earlobe. *He bit me*. His teeth drag over delicate flesh. The wet heat of his mouth raises goose bumps. I gasp.

I want him to do it again. And again. And lower. I want to smell the musk and motor oil and old leather scent that clings to his body, and feel his rough stubble scrape over my belly. I want— I jerk without letting go of the bar.

"Your hands?" He nuzzles into my ear on the question. And I can only nod. Mind racing. *My hands. Yes. My hands. What should I do with my hands?* "They go around my waist. Try to keep 'em off my dick while I'm driving."

Shock, shame, arousal—I am dizzy and denied.

He slips the helmet over my head, and everything goes dark. My world is quiet and still until he settles on the bike in front of me. I wrap my arms around him and carefully link my fingers together just above his belt buckle, anchoring myself to his body.

There is panic in this darkness, but it pulses between my legs and mingles with the vibration from the engine. It soothes as it savages.

Noah.

I realize I never told him where to find Harry and he never asked.

I have no idea where he's taking me or what he's planning to do with me when we get there.

Oh, but I hope.

FIVE

I sit on the back of the bike with my eyes closed long after he's gotten off. I'm in no hurry to find out where we are or what will happen next. We could be at some seedy bar or a meth lab or worse—the middle of nowhere. My brain says that would be worse, but my heart flutters like it might be the best thing ever. A sccluded spot...just the two of us. I don't even care. It's all out of my control, and for the first time in a long time I feel free. Which is stupid since I am possibly the most not-free I've ever been.

Snap. "Off."

It takes me a second to register that the noise I heard was fingers snapping, that those fingers must belong to Noah, and that he'd commanded me *off* his bike like an unruly pet. A fresh burst of indignity courses through me, and I slip off the leather seat, tearing at the helmet as I go. A gust of cool night air raises goose bumps along my sweat-damp neck.

Noah smirks at my graceless dismount, and I swallow my anger. I'm too busy taking in the familiar street behind him, houses like salt boxes stacked beside each other with little strips of scraggly grass between them. I hop over the cracks in the driveway beneath our feet every single day. I know if I turn around, I'll see the weathered steps that lead up to my garage apartment.

"Is this some kind of joke? You drove me home? How the hell do you even know where I live?" My heart thumps heavy in my chest, and I'm not sure if what I'm feeling is panic that he knew where I lived all along or disappointment that he hasn't whisked me away…yet. There's that dangerous hope—spurring me on, turning the sharp twist of dread into a caress.

"Sweetheart, I'm an enforcer for the Devil's Host. I didn't roll up on Harry without knowing exactly what I was walking into tonight, right down to what color panties Jimmy prefers you girls wear under your new uniforms."

"So why didn't you just wait out back for Harry?"

"I needed to know what he'd do if I came for him like a man. It doesn't matter anymore if he's got Dev's money or not...he ran. He can't be trusted. Now I'll track him like an animal."

The fire in my belly turns to ice as my worst fears for Harry are confirmed, and I whisper, "I didn't run."

His lip curls up into a crooked smile that makes my knees wobble even though I'm scared. His eyes flash mischief and something else, something that in another man I might think was regret. "You haven't been given the opportunity."

His hand darts out, and then—*crack*—my ass is hot. Pain, heat, pleasure—they're all mixed up together, and I can hardly believe it. I reach back to cup the assaulted cheek, to soothe and protect it. To hold that feeling in for as long as I can.

He laughs. "Now go on home, little girl. It's past your bedtime, and I've got work to do that I'm sure you don't have the stomach for."

I should feel relief, but all I feel is hurt. "You were going to take me home all along, weren't you? All that big bad was an act?"

"Big and bad is who I am, Star. That's the job description. I like watching you squirm, but fuck, this just…seems like the right thing to do. Don't test me."

"Do you always do the right thing?" I hold my breath, waiting for the answer.

"Almost never."

I take a step forward and touch my fingertips to the belt buckle I'd been holding on to during our ride. I want it to burn me, but it doesn't. "What if I want you to chase me?"

"I promise you don't. And sweetheart, what you want doesn't factor into this equation."

I wonder if what *he* wants factors in at all. I slip my hand below his belt buckle and skim my palm over the erection straining against his jeans. I know what he wants.

He clamps a hand over mine, stilling it, and his breath fans hot against my ear. "You're playing with matches."

"I'm playing with you."

And then his lips are on mine. He licks into my mouth like a brush fire, hot and crazy, and I can barely stay standing. Tongue and teeth and rough hands pushing up under my skirt. I'd spread for him right here in the driveway, let him burn me to the ground until I'm nothing but a smudge of ash on the pavement.

The kiss doesn't slow down or taper off; it just stops. He yanks back and leaves me reeling. "Now's your chance, Star."

Dizzy, I touch my hand to my buzzing mouth like it might anchor me. "My what?"

His eyes look darker, lust drunk and heavy-lidded. A lazy predator. He doesn't smile. He bares his teeth.

"Run."

Whatever that thing is that makes animals head for high ground an hour before an earthquake, I don't have it. I don't get out of danger early, ever. But my fight-or-flight response works on overdrive, finely honed by years of disasters. I stumble backward to get away before he's finished curling his tongue into the *n* sound. I fucking run.

But my feet and my back hurt, and the adrenaline from the incident with Officer Wade is wearing off. Was that really only half an hour ago? Not even. Doesn't matter. I kick off my heels. The hose are ruined anyway. Ripped open in a way no amount of nail polish could ever fix. I'm pretty sure *I'm* ruined.

My palms leave sweaty blotches on the trunk of my landlord's ancient Caddy when I push off to dart toward my steps, and then my legs are out from under me. Two hot bolts zing from the heels of my hands up to my elbows. My palms take the brunt of the fall, which seems fitting since they're to blame. A choked sound startles me, and I realize it's coming from my throat. From me. I'm making this muffled keening noise and crying a little bit, and he hasn't even moved.

I'm crab crawling backward across the driveway, totally overwhelmed, operating completely on instinct, and Noah's a damn statue. Just as cold. Just as beautiful.

He ran. He can't be trusted.

Noah's words from before tumble up to the surface of my churning thoughts, and I freeze. I don't want to run away from him, even if I should. Even if he's telling me to do just that. I already know he wants me, but I want him to trust me—to need me. That thought terrifies me, and I mentally revise my desires. Who could need me? I just want him to fuck me. That's all.

Maybe I *don't* have enough sense to come in out of the rain. Maybe that's why I'm waitressing in East Dead End and saving my money by shoving singles and fives into a Folgers can instead of a bank account. Maybe every awful thing anyone has ever said about me is true. *Stupid girl*. *Fucking tramp*. *Lazy bitch*.

I don't care. None of that matters or makes me...me. I'm exhausted, and Noah's mouth on mine is better than ten cups of coffee.

He crosses the driveway in a few long strides, bends over and scoops me up. "That was some half-assed running."

His voice is rough velvet, and I want to wrap it around me like a blanket. I press my face into his chest instead and hope he doesn't care that my wet cheeks are soaking his leather. "My heart wasn't in it."

"Anything else I tell you to do, you fucking do it." It's almost a plea, and I wonder for a second if, beneath his marble surface, he's feeling half as desperate as I am.

Desperate or not. Command or plea. Either way, I know he means it. And I mean it too when I nod in agreement. I'll do anything he asks me to do except run away from him. Not because he's good and kind and carrying me to the safety of my apartment. But because he's none of those things and he's doing it anyway.

He carries me up the rickety steps, and I don't even flinch when he kicks the door in instead of asking me for the keys. It seems perfectly natural.

Right even. Why would he use keys like a normal person?

The faint wet-dog scent of my threadbare carpet greets us. *Home sweet home.* No candle, powder, or spray can ever really cover it. Usually I'd feel shame having someone smell the filth I live in, but not with Noah. That seems right too.

We can wallow together.

"Behind the curtain." I point toward the beaded curtain that separates my sleeping area from the rest of the living space.

He grunts and takes me to bed.

At least my sheets are clean. That's my last coherent thought before he climbs in after me and presses the length of his body against mine. Lining us up so we are mouth to mouth. His fingers slide into my hair, and I sigh at the massaging touch, moan at the pinch and pull when he tangles it up into his fist. He works his other hand between us, trailing it up my inner thigh, opening the run further, finding his way to the soaked center of my panties and shoving them aside. I'm so wet I can hear the slipping noises as he invades me with blunt fingers. Teasing, searching and plunging. I buck against him, arching off the bed at the pleasure building sharp and sweet where his thumb is circling my clit.

My palms still sting where I scraped them, but I grab fistfuls of blanket anyway because I have to hold on to something. This is nothing like the lazy touch I use to bring myself to an easy finish. Or the fumbling pluck of so many other lovers, searching—and missing—as if my pleasure is difficult to find. I don't have to shift my hips and guide him. He's going to make me come hard and fast in seconds with nothing but his thumb and forefinger. Like he wrote my fucking manual. Easy as cake.

And I'd hate him for wringing these feelings from my body so easily if they weren't so damn delicious.

He licks at my mouth again, and it's so much more than kissing. It's tasting—teasing. "Star?"

"Yes, yes." I pant against him. All I can say is yes. Yeses that mean *finish me off, fuck me, do what you want.* Yes. My whole world is spinning in the palm of his hand right now, beyond wet and past ready.

"If we do this. If I fuck you. If I take you with me…"

"If…?"

He scrapes his stubble over my cheek, abrading me. Marking me. The edge of orgasm shimmers just beyond my reach, pinpricks of light through dark water. *If. If. If.* I am drowning and breathing and—

"You're mine."

He pulls me taut like a bowstring, and I snap, pleasure radiating out in waves. "Oh God. I think I'm coming."

"If you're thinking, you're not coming." He thumbs my clit harder, cruel strokes that have me jerking against him. "You wouldn't be my old lady; this isn't about love. This is about survival. Understand?"

I want to tell him to shut up, that I don't care, that he shouldn't be telling me this while my pussy is rippling around his fingers. But it would all be lies and he'd know it. And then I'm breaking hard over the edge of bliss. No thinking. No understanding. Only being. "Yessss."

He pulls free of my body, and suddenly his fingers are in my mouth, slick with my juices and pungent with my own flavor—familiar and strange. "Lick them clean, baby."

My cheeks burn and my clit throbs as I suck every last drop of myself from his fingers, hollowing my cheeks and swirling my tongue.

Like a good girl.

"You wouldn't be Star anymore. You'd be Noah's woman."

His fingers stay in my mouth when he wraps himself around me on the small bed.

We lay like that for a long time—fully clothed, fully aroused...cuddling? Is that what this is? As ridiculous as it seems, the answer is yes...almost.

Whatever it is, it isn't enough. If I'm going to be his, why isn't he taking me? I wriggle my ass against the hard length of his erection in a lewd invitation.

He slips free of my mouth and clamps his hand down on my hip. "Be still. We'll fuck when I'm ready. Right now we're going to sleep."

Burning up with wanting, desperate for more, I stuff it all down. I let the exhaustion I've been battling overtake me. I do as I'm told.

SIX

I wake up to late morning sunlight slanting through metal blinds and Noah's hard body still burning behind me. He rolls us over so I'm straddling him on my creaky twin bed. It's just a mattress and box spring on a metal frame, there's no headboard or footboard to anchor it in place, and it sounds like something off a Halloween sound-effects tape. If he fucks me hard and fast, the way I want him to, it'll leave gouges in the floor. I want that. I want to mark this shitty apartment so the next time my landlord is snooping around, pawing through my things, probably jerking off into my dirty laundry, he'll know someone else was here. That my life is my own.

My dress is bunched up around my waist, and Noah yanks it higher. "Take this off. I want to see all of you while you ride me."

Lust burns away the haze of sleep. I've never been on top before, but I've seen it in movies, imagined what it would be like…exposed and awkward. In control. I fumble with the zipper at my back and peel the awful uniform off my body. At the last second I do a little shimmy, twirl the dress lasso-style, and fling it across the room. "Like this?"

"Just like that." Noah's smile is the eye of a storm. Bright sunshine in the middle of a hurricane. Unlikely and unsettling in its perfection. "Gimme a show."

My whole body lights up with his approval. "I'll try."

I unhook my bra, and I'm not even worried that it's one of the sturdy ones I always wear for work, dingy gray from too many trips through the wash with jeans before I learned to rinse them in the sink and hang them over the shower rod. He's looking at me like I'm wearing one of the laciest negligees I ever saw while window-shopping at Victoria's Secret. His hungry gaze is sexier on my skin than any silk or satin I could've grabbed off the clearance rack.

The wide straps slip down my arms, and my breasts, finally freed, ache to be touched. As if the bastard can read my mind, Noah tucks his hands behind his head. Denying me, making me suffer. He'd said it outside; he likes to watch me squirm. He'd said it just now. *He wants to watch.*

I've never been so turned on in my life, so I cup my own breasts. I imagine how they'd feel to him. Soft. Smooth. I flick my thumbs over tight nipples and test their weight—heavy. Spurred on by his grunts of approval and the sparks of pleasure, I knead them with my palms. Squeeze them cruelly the way he would. When I pinch my nipples, he lifts his hips off the bed.

"It's a crime you're not topless all the time. Perfect. Fucking. Breasts. I'm gonna come all over them later. What are you thinking about while you play with them? Tell me."

Every inch of my skin is already blushing, yet somehow I pulse hotter. My cheeks. My chest. I feel heavy, like my blood is thicker than normal, like there's more gravity in the room simply because he's in it. Maybe there is. It draws words out of my mouth I didn't even know I had in me. "You. I'm thinking about your greedy hands all over me. Rough and dirty. How you'd pinch and tug and take. How you'd fuck me up."

"That what you want?"

His cock is hard behind denim, and I grind down on it. My pussy is still so wet and sensitive, I think I could come again just like this with a few jerks of my hips—rocking against the rough fabric trapping his erection. "Unnh. You know it is."

He hooks an arm around me and crushes me against his chest. I can hardly breathe from the shock of it. He grabs my ass with one hand and the back of my head with the other, pressing my face into his shoulder. I'm trapped in his embrace, spread open and pinned. "I know you—people like you. Hanging around the club, looking for…something. What are you looking for?"

Chest to chest, his voice rumbles through me. I jerk against him, desperate for that friction, the bite of his zipper against my clit. Anything.

"I don't know." I lie.

Somewhere distant I hear a bang and realize it's the front door caught in the wind. The door he kicked in is hanging from its hinges, and so am I.

I bite his shoulder to keep myself from begging him to fuck me already. Or to let me fuck him. I struggle to break free—to do just that—but he squeezes me tighter. Pinches my ass with those greedy hands I'm so desperate for. It's almost enough to tip me over the edge. "God, please—"

"Whatever you're running from? I'm not a way out. I'm a fucking self-destruct button."

"That's exactly what I want." I grind down harder—as hard as possible with what little leverage I can manage—and this time the friction *is* pain. A sharp bolt, flashing bright white behind my eyes and fading into something so bone-deep good I'd risk any hurt to feel it again and again. "Fuuuck. This apartment, this life? It's not worth anything. We can tear it all down."

"We?" His sigh, heavy and tired, rolls over me. A different kind of bone-deep, like I've said the wrong thing. And it's the same wrong thing he's heard a hundred times before. He grips my shoulders and pushes me up.

I watch his mouth while he talks, barely hearing the words as they trip over the disgusted sneer curling his lips. "You mean me. Usually I get paid to fuck shit up. We could work something out."

Somehow I'm smoothing over that snarl, tracing the edges of his mouth where softest skin meets scruff, willing it back to the stormy smile with the tips of my fingers. The smile that left me frightened and giddy. I want that one again.

I don't know if he hates what he thinks I want from him or if he hates who he is. But I know he hates something, and I can understand either way. Sometimes I've got so much hate inside me it's a wonder there's room for anything else. It's an awful feeling, and I wouldn't wish it on my worst enemy. "Not like arson or vandalism. I don't mean literally."

His eyes are flat mirrors as I study him. Reflecting nothing and everything. "I do. Did you forget why I'm here?"

"No." I lie again. Two lies in one morning and I think I'm only getting started. At least they're transparent and utterly pointless. I'm not really lying, not really hiding anything, just preserving some false shred of modesty.

I *had* forgotten why he was here, in town, in my apartment, in my bed. For hours while we slept. For long seconds while his fingers raked over my clit and that other spot deep inside me, the one that felt like a self-destruct button too, he existed only to make me feel. Each stroke dragged me closer to the abyss.

God, I want him to touch me again, screw modesty. I grab his hands from their resting place on my thigh and pull them up to my breasts.

"Look at you. One little taste and you don't want to stop. Just say no to drugs, sweet girl. I could have you strung out and working the corner in a fucking heartbeat. Is that the kind of destruction you're begging for?"

Adrenaline spikes my bloodstream, the butterflies in my belly turning into bats that swoop and whirl and scream into the night. Because this is something I've thought about, many times. Not so much the drugs, because he's right. One taste and I probably would be done for. That particular sweet tooth isn't just a thread of family history; it's rooted deep in my DNA from every side. But the other part...the part where I might take money for sex.

I've been hungry and alone. There were times I felt so disconnected from my body that I thought it might not even matter who touched me. Fifteen minutes of tugging or grinding and... I shake my head. I get by. It's what I do. The only thing that separated me from the girls that sometimes wandered between trucks in the parking lot at Jimmy's before they put in the bypass was that stupid coffee can of savings under my sink and a twist of fate. "Is that what you do when you're not being an enforcer? Are you a...pimp?"

He tenses beneath me. Flinches. Before he so much as tilts his chin in my direction, I know the answer is no. This was just more posturing.

He squeezes his eyes shut. "I can't shock you, can I?"

"It's not all an act—I'm not stupid, but I bet you could shock me more if you stopped trying so hard to scare me away."

"Fine." He takes a long look at my body, up and down and back up again. A searching gaze that tightens my nipples and raises the blush that had started to recede. Every flick of his eyes feels like a puzzle piece being snapped into place. "Suck me off."

"What?" I'd expected him to argue with me, to be even bigger and badder, to bang his chest and prove me wrong. Waitressing taught me to read people pretty well, but maybe I'd miscalculated. I roll off him and stand beside the bed.

Ooof. I stumble when his hand snakes between my legs and around my thigh, pinning me before I can't get more than a step away.

"You heard me. You want me to stop trying to scare you away? Get to work. Put that perceptive little mouth of yours on my cock. I've been imagining what it would feel like since you hit your knees outside the diner."

Somewhere in the back of my brain I know I'm supposed to be a little pissed off, but I'm too busy wondering if he can feel the wetness running down the inside of my thigh and thinking about how fucking hot it sounds. "Yes, sir."

"Don't call me sir. That's for bankers and businessmen and shit. Boring fucks who wear ties and drive Volvos." He flicks open the fly of his jeans while he scolds me, and his heavy palm pushing down on my shoulder lets me know I'm obliged to perform from the floor, not the bed.

He stands up, and I keep my eyes trained on the open flap of his pants, the navy cotton underwear peeking out, the erection barely contained by either. "I call everyone sir at work."

"This ain't work."

Well, that settles one thing. I tug the pants down from his hips and suck in a breath. The ink swirling over his hands and arms swirls over his belly too. Every inch of him that I can see is covered. Except the lowest part of his abdomen...and his cock. Thick and blunt and glistening with pre-cum. Oh, that cock could hurt me. It could choke me. It might do both of those things before our time together is over. I squeeze my thighs together at the thought, because damn if that isn't exactly what I want.

"You're squirming and licking your lips, Star. Tell me what's going on in that busy head of yours or get to it."

The silky skin of his dick is so hot against my palm. I curl my fingers around the base and squeeze once before licking the tip with the flat of my tongue, catching the salty drops beaded there and whisking them away. I lap at the underside, slicking him from the base of his cock to the ridge beneath the head—and look up at him. For approval? For reassurance? For instruction? I don't know. For something.

His eyes are shuttered, offering me absolutely nothing. So I push. I tell him what I'm thinking between lazy licks. "Your cock's gonna hurt me. That's what I was thinking."

"No, sweetheart. *I'm* going to hurt you. And you like that, don't you? Shit. I tried to hold back, but you just won't let me, will you?" He wraps my hair in his hand and pushes me down.

I open my mouth instinctively, taking the hot length of him between my lips. This is what I want. This invasion.

"I'm going to get so deep inside you—your mouth, your pussy, your mind." He rocks his hips, nudging his cock deeper still.

I try to take it, but no amount of slow deep breathing can stop the reflex that makes my throat spasm and my shoulders hitch. He grunts, tightening his fingers in my hair, and I know he likes that too. Likes me on my knees, choking for him. Likes me whimpering. He pumps faster, and my eyes water. Fuck, he's big. I try to pull back, to shorten the strokes a little, but his hand is on the back of my head, pulling my hair, urging me to take more. To take everything he gives me. Forcing me.

My clit throbs. I slip a hand between my legs, and he grunts his approval.

"That's it, baby. Get yourself off while I fuck your face."

Yes.

My body answers with an orgasm that breaks like the tide, an angry wave against a rocky shore. Hard and fast. Inevitable. I shudder, but my cries are trapped at the back of my throat, muffled against his cock.

I'm coming. I'm coming so hard. All over my hand, on the floor in front of him. I feel ruined and perfect. Powerful, desperate and spent. I feel everything at once.

He jerks free of my mouth and pumps himself, painting hot come across my neck and breasts. Just like he promised earlier. *I'm going to come all over them.*

He swirls a finger in the mess he's made—a quick flourish that could be a figure eight even if it does feel like a heart—and swipes it over my bottom lip. "When I'm through with you, I promise you're going to ache for days and there won't be an inch of you left that isn't mine."

When I'm through with you...

Oh, the sweetness and the sorrow. I'm starting to realize Noah keeps his promises.

SEVEN

The front door slams again, and this time it's followed by heavy footsteps that rattle the floor under my knees. I jerk back to grab the comforter off the bed—to cover myself—but Noah stops me. With one hand he cups the back of my head and presses my face to his thigh. The gesture feels possessive, protective and almost tender. The reassuring stroke of his thumb against my scalp, up and down, makes me shiver.

It shouldn't. I should be terrified and embarrassed. Adrenaline should be pumping fresh in my veins, but I've got nothing left. I'm naked, on my knees and covered in come, while someone I don't know storms into my apartment, and my heartbeat barely trips.

Noah's other hand is wrapped around a flat-black gun. Something stubby and squat and so much a part of him I barely noticed when he slipped it from the back of his pants and deposited it on my nightstand last night. I notice it now, even if I only see it for a second before he turns his upper body toward the door. I notice his pointer finger on the trigger, imagine that reassuring stroke.

Under my arms, the muscles in his tree-trunk legs are tense. "You following me now, brother? I don't remember asking for a babysitter."

Brother? I don't think he means the blood kind. Maybe the *blood oath* kind.

"Yeah, I'm following you. Followed you here last night, sure as shit didn't expect to find you here this morning. You got a death wish? That bitch better be polishing your wood so you can build an ark, Noah. Dev's about to rain a world of hurt down on you for going off the grid."

Bitch barely touches me. I've been called worse by people I actually care about. *Dev* sends a chill down my spine, though. It's Dev's money Harry ran off with. Dev is the reason Noah sat in my section vibrating with barely contained menace and smoldering attitude.

I strain to listen.

Noah's voice is as flat as the finish on his gun. "I'm going to pretend you didn't bust in here uninvited using such a disrespectful tone. Otherwise I'd be obligated to teach you some fucking manners."

"Whoa, whoa, don't shoot the messenger. I wouldn't even be here if you'd check your damn phone. We've got a job to do."

"Following me *and* telling me my job? Damn, Stone. You want to help this honey suck my dick too?"

Honey stings. Like a rubber band snapped against my wrist, reminding me of my place. But sweeter because it's followed by the slide of his palm over my hair. The gesture could just be an invitation to Stone, but I don't care.

For several long seconds silence stretches between them and my pulse finally catches up with the very real danger in the room, thumping away in a staccato beat that has me imagining the pop-pop-pop of gunshots.

"Fuck you, you fucking fuck." Stone laughs.

When Noah laughs in response, the tension spooling in my chest unwinds. He lowers his weapon as the gruff sound, harsh and already familiar, shakes through him. The hand he's kept buried in my hair finally stills. Had he been comforting me or taking comfort?

He draws me up, keeping himself between me and Stone but forcing me to stand. I cling more tightly to the shield of his body.

Hot breath whispers over my ear. "No turning back now, sweet girl." His words tumble in a rush—rough, tender, just for me. "Remember what I said. You're mine. Nobody fucks with what's mine."

His lips brush my forehead, so soft and sweet it almost hurts. I nod, and he steps back, exposing me. The shift from softness to snarling is a shock.

"Go clean yourself up, bitch. We've got business to discuss."

This time *bitch* hits me like a slap, even though I know it's more for Stone's benefit than mine. Know? Assume. Shit. I don't *know* one damn thing.

I scramble to cover my breasts with my hands, all the shame I hadn't had time to feel suddenly slamming into me, bending my body and burning it up from the inside out.

Stone whistles through his teeth. "Niiiiice. Bringing Dev a souvenir will go a long way to getting back in his good graces."

Is that what I am? A souvenir? A party favor to be passed around? No. The memory of Noah's touch washes over me. Greedy and possessive. The breath from his whispered instructions still clings to my skin. *Mine.*

63

I grab some clothes from my dresser and head to the bathroom, clutching soft cotton and denim to my front. Noah slaps my ass as I go. The heat of his palm, another sharp reminder. A reassurance.

"I haven't decided."

Is that a threat or a promise? My knuckles are white gripping the scuffed brass doorknob. I'm torn—frozen on the threshold by fear and desire. A terrible thought rolls over and over in my mind, a foolish and stupid thought, one I should not be having as two men with guns discuss the value of my ass to their boss.

He can't be done with me yet.

Do I want him to be?

Stone snorts. "You think you have a choice?"

Stone is talking to Noah, but it feels like he's speaking directly to me. *You think you have a choice?* Every syllable strokes something inside me—scratching over a terrible itch I've never been able to reach. And when I dare a glance at Noah's face, I know the answer. His jaw flexes and he gives Stone the same hard glare he gave me when Officer Wade interrupted us last night. I won't have a choice in whatever happens next. Maybe I never really did. Not when he told me to run, not when he protected me back at the diner. Noah has been in charge from the second he filled up the doorway to the diner. Leading me toward this moment.

"Let's go," he says, this time softly, only for me. *What if I don't want to go?*

But I don't want to be left behind either. I open my mouth and close it without speaking. Because there's nothing to say. Nothing to ask. Not with words.

Our eyes lock and for a moment it feels like we're equals. Both uncertain. Both just trying to get by. Then he shakes his head. "Too late for that. I can't leave you here when you're connected to Harry. You're in too deep now."

"So she *is* connected." Stone whistles through his teeth again. "I thought maybe you were on a little fuck-cation. I shoulda known you were taking Harry's debt out in trade. Dev won't appreciate you skimming your cut off the top but he'll be glad you were working."

"You keep your damn mouth shut, Stone. Dev will get his."

The room spins and I can hardly breathe. *Trade. Debt.* "I—I—can't pay Harry's debt. I don't have that kind of money."

Noah smirks. "You know money isn't the only way we get paid."

"Oh God. So all of the touching and grabbing and claiming? All of that was to pay a debt? How about the spooning? Was that to pay a debt too?" My face flames and I can't control the rush of an-

65

gry words pouring out of me. "How much did I earn with your fingers inside me? How much for sucking your cock? You bastard. You said you weren't a pimp."

"Did I say that? I don't think I did."

Didn't he? I try to remember if he'd actually denied it or if I'd just assumed. How many other blanks had I filled in wrong?

"You said it wasn't work."

I hate how small my voice has gotten—barely more than a squeak. My throat is so tight if I tried to make a bigger sound I might rip something loose or burst into tears. I refuse to do that. I will not lose my shit in front of them.

His gaze softens. "Did it feel like work?"

All I can do is shake my head because it hadn't felt like work. It hadn't felt like anything I'd ever experienced before. But I know better. I swallow around a lump thc size of a softball and force myself to speak. "The way things feel and the way they are, are two very different things."

"Smart girl." Noah closes the distance between us and grabs a handful of my hair in his fist. I gasp, shocked by the sudden movement, but his touch is nearly tender. There's no sting at my scalp, only at my pride. "Now listen close. I said you were *mine*. That's all that fucking matters. And you're coming whether you like it or not because I take care of what's mine. Now dry your eyes and get dressed or I'm putting you on the back of my bike naked."

BREAK ME IN

PART 2 OF 4

ONE

I look back at my garage apartment one last time and worry for a second that I'll turn into a pillar of salt right here in the driveway.

The busted front door hangs crooked from the hinges at the top of the rickety steps. *Noah did that in his rush to have me.* It's a stunning display of devastation and desire. As I walk toward Noah's bike, I picture my landlord's face, purple with rage, when he discovers the destruction. I wonder if he'll think something terrible happened to me or if he'll just be happy I'm gone. *The bastard.* I should've known anyone who'd rent to a teenager with no references, no bank account and no security deposit was probably not someone who'd value my privacy or honor the terms of a lease. God, I hadn't even known I was supposed to have a lease.

But I'd managed. And he hadn't even started to give me a hard time about anything until I realized that he wasn't supposed to come and go from my place as he pleased. When I finally asked him for a lease last year, he'd laughed in my face. The next time I brought him the rent a few hours late, he'd already printed an eviction notice. I got the message loud and clear: there'd be no more second chances.

I can almost feel the lump of cash I'd slipped from my coffee can on the way out the door burning like a hot coal in my bag. Not quite enough for the rent due next week. Nowhere near enough for first and last on a new place.

Certainly not enough to buy my freedom. There's never enough for that, no matter how many shifts I work.

Sure, I've managed. But I haven't done much more than that. Almost three years in that shithole and now I'm not managing at all. It's probably stupid and dangerous to have all my cash with me, but there isn't a chance in hell I'll leave it behind.

I don't know when I'll be back. *If* I'll be back. But most of all, I don't know why I stayed so long.

"It's not too late to strip you naked again and throw you over my shoulder. Get your sweet ass on this bike." Noah says but I don't falter.

"Does a topless ride through town earn me anything extra? Is there a rate card somewhere I can consult?" I slip behind him.

Stone adjusts his sunglasses. "She's a fucking handful."

Noah reaches back and claps a hand on my leg, digs his fingers into the thin denim stretched over my generous thigh, and squeezes. "More than."

I know by the sureness of his touch and the pleasure in his voice that it's a compliment.

Noah and Stone both rev their engines in the driveway, but we don't pull away. The sound is loud and forbidding, two snarling beasts, and I see a few blinds snap open across the street. This isn't the kind of neighborhood where people will help if there's trouble, but they'll peek through their curtains and maybe call the cops if it looks like someone is loading a TV into the back of a shady truck.

They'll leave *me* to my fate, though. If they even notice at all. It's not like I'm a brand-new flat screen.

It's still better than the neighborhood I grew up in. In that kind of neighborhood people stay far away from the windows if they think there's trouble. One like where Harry lives now. Or lived. *Shit, where the hell is that son of a bitch?* I feel the butt of Noah's gun through his jacket and shiver. People sure as shit don't call for help in neighborhoods like that. Help only ever makes things worse. They call for revenge, street justice, the kind found tucked into the waistband of Noah's jeans.

A car the color of my landlord's caddy slows down as it rolls by, and I squeeze closer to Noah, press my face into the leather stretched across his back and take a steadying breath. "Get me out of here."

Before he comes home for an early lunch raving about destruction of property or disorderly conduct and tells me not to come back. I don't say any of that out loud because I'm not ready to seal my fate just yet. I know I may not have a home to come back to, but Noah doesn't need to know that.

I swallow down the *please* that's ready to trip off my tongue. I don't have to ask him to do something I already know he's going to do.

"It's cute how you think you're calling the shots." Noah says.

He's taking me out of here as payment for a debt. And for my own good. Supposedly to protect me from Stone. I study the man beside us out of the corner of my eye. He and Noah are two sides of the same coin, large and intimidating, covered in ink and leather.

But Noah makes me feel safe, even when I'm terrified. And as much as he warns me not to trust him, I can't help it. He saved me from Officer Wade. He's protected me with his fists and shielded me with his body. He's the devil I know.

I curl my fingers around his belt buckle. "Does it cost you anything to let me pretend I've got a little control?"

He laughs. "That kind of delusion is expensive, but I think I can afford it."

We lurch, and then the tires grip the road and we're off.

Wrapped around him, flying through the streets on the back of his motorcycle with nothing between me and a fiery death on the pavement but the wind and a promise...I've never felt more alive.

TWO

I'm surprised when we slow down after only for-ty-five minutes. For some reason I'd expected the drive to be long, imagined wherever we were going had to be far, far away. As if we were in some de-mented fairy tale. My black knight on his black horse whisking me off to a darker realm. But we're just two towns over. Two exits beyond the bypass choking the life out of Jimmy's Diner.

A blip on the map. More of the same.

We pull into a run-down strip mall. A Laun-dromat props up one end, with a handful of pa-trons visible through the foggy window. A curl of fabric-softener-scented steam drifts beyond the front door and overpowers the leather and exhaust surrounding me. Next to the Laundromat is a tiny pet store, long closed. All in Pawn seems to be doing well with its neon OPEN sign and sleek music equipment on display. Somebody's dream deferred or abandoned for God knows what. A rent check, a sick kid... And Patty's Clip 'n' Curl props up the other end. Pink paint peels off the brick facade, making me think of makeup left on overnight.

Stone hops off his bike. "You take Luca, and I'll go see Patty. Let's do this quick. I want to head back to the club sooner rather than later. The longer Dev waits, the more fucked-up he gets."

Noah doesn't make a move. "I'm not taking her into Luca's."

"It's a pawn shop, not a porn studio."

"He's a pig. The last time I collected there, I had to break his nose."

"This time shouldn't be a problem then, but leave her to wait by the bikes if you're worried."

"You got a leash on you? I'll just tie her to the handle bar while we go do our business." Noah's voice drips with sarcasm, but Stone doesn't seem to care. A mistake on Stone's part, for sure.

Stone leans in close to me and rests his hand on my shoulder. I force myself not to jerk away. "You're not going anywhere, are you, kitten? You know what would happen—"

And then Noah is moving. He's a wall of angry muscle, and I hang on to the bike to keep from getting hauled along with him. "Hands. Off. Unless you want to lose them."

Stone raises both offending hands palms out and backs away slowly, grinning ear to ear. "Come on, brother. You got yourself a taste this morning. Patty's real friendly. And real grateful for our protection."

"Maybe if you knew her name wasn't actually Patty, I'd let you take this one. Patty was her grandmother, you dipshit."

Stone sneers. "Sorry, we don't have coffee and chat about extended family."

"Attention to detail, *brother.* Pay enough and it'll get you laid. Too little and it'll get you dead. Look around. It's a Saturday morning. There should be a line of old ladies here to get their weekend frizz on. What's up with that? "

"There's a sale on Ensure at the A&P?"

Noah shakes his head. "Go bang on Luca until some change falls out." Then he turns to me. "Come on, baby. You want to get your hair done?"

The question is so ridiculous I don't even know how to respond. "What? Why?"

"No customers means no money in the register. She's gotta pay one way or another, and I'm not having her do for me what Stone was after."

"You mean sex."

He nods.

"If I wasn't with you?"

He runs a hand through his dark hair and smirks. "I wouldn't be getting a trim."

Bells tinkle above the door as we enter the shop, and a dark-haired woman in her thirties peers over her magazine. Her lips are so chapped it looks painful. When she licks them nervously, I understand why. "That time again already?"

"Where'd all your customers go, Kristi?"

"Luca's been causing some trouble. I don't think he's very discriminating about the type of merchandise he's willing to buy lately. It brings the wrong sort of clientele to the mall. There's times I don't even want to cross the parking lot by myself, but what's a girl to do?"

"You could've called. This is the kind of shit we're here for. Protection."

Her face twists in confusion. "Dev came by and told me to keep my mouth shut and my eyes on my magazines. I'm doing it, but damn. I don't just pay you bastards. The bank's on my ass too, and they won't take a blow job in payment." Her pretty brown eyes fill with tears that don't fall, and she twirls a manicured hand at the empty salon. "Wouldn't my nana be so proud?"

"Your nana was a good woman who did what needed to be done to provide for you. She was a friend of the club, and that means something."

"But Dev—"

"I'll take care of him. Now take care of Star. Whatever she wants. If I'm going to tell the brothers they need to send their old ladies up here, we need to sample the merchandise."

He nudges me forward, and I squirm under their scrutiny. "Maybe just a trim. I haven't had one of those in a while."

"Honey, your split ends have split ends."

"I've been busy."

Kristi looks from me to Noah and back again and purses her sore lips. "Yeah, I get that."

Warm water rushes over my scalp, soaking my hair. I scoot back farther in the reclining chair, letting my head fall deeper into the shampoo bowl so the water doesn't run down the back of my neck.

"Too hot?" Kristi asks, pulling the stream away.

"No, it's perfect. I was just getting comfortable."

Kristi lifts the bulk of my hair and directs the spray underneath. "You relax. I'll take good care of you."

"Mhmmm," I murmur as she works up a coconut-scented lather. Her touch is brisk and efficient.

In minutes I'm reduced to jelly. I wonder if it would be too forward to ask her to work her magic on the small of my back. "That feels so nice. I don't think there's anything more decadent than having someone wash your hair."

Then her tight circles are replaced by broad strokes, and I gasp. My eyes flutter open, and Noah is hovering over me.

"The noises you were making? All those mmms and aaahs? I only want to hear them if I'm the one wringing them out of your body." He glides soapy fingers along my neck and trails them over my collar bone. Cool water runs down my breasts, soaking my shirt and tightening my nipples. My cheeks burn and I squeeze my eyes shut.

"I'll take a break in the back room. Don't forget the conditioner." Kristi says.

"Don't go far." Noah grunts and continues massaging me, working his way ever so slowly back to my scalp.

The spray starts back up, and I hear a break in the stream before it lands on my soapy tresses. The realization that he checked the temperature warms me more than the water.

"I'm not going to fuck you here, Star. Not in Kristi's shop. She's put up with enough. But I had to get my hands on you again. If anyone is making you feel good, I want it to be me." He tugs my hair, pulling me taut, and flicks his tongue over my mouth. I feel deprived and pleased all at once. There are things he's not willing to do, boundaries he won't cross. More ways to pay than just with a body. "I'm going to have some words with Luca. I'll be back to collect you."

I wonder if words means broken bones. I wonder but I don't ask, because Kristi is back with her magic fingers and a rich conditioner. I'm careful not to make a sound, though. Not because it doesn't feel good, but because Noah made it clear. All my moans belong to him.

I can give him that.

THREE

We pull into a fenced lot and park next to a long line of bikes in front of a warehouse. I assume it's a warehouse with its corrugated metal walls and windows up near the roofline.

Noah's muscles are tense. He'd softened under my touch on the road, but here, he's wound up tight. I run my palms over his back in soothing circles, let my fingers play over the patches stitched to the leather and wait for him to make a move.

Stone gets off his bike first. "Give me your phone, Romeo."

Noah slips his phone out of a pocket inside his jacket and tosses it to Stone.

Stone drops it on the ground and slams his boot heel into the shiny screen. It's a sick crunch, and plastic pieces fly everywhere. Noah growls. "What the fuck are you doing?"

"Saving your ass. Again. Now you can tell Dev your phone is busted. You're welcome."

Noah scoops up the biggest pieces and presses them into my hand. "Hang on to these for me. There's a SIM card in there somewhere."

I follow them toward the building's entrance. A large dog lopes near us but Noah snaps his fingers and it turns away. Muted sounds filter out beyond the door, and my belly flips. I can't tell if that's music or shouting. I have no idea what's on the other side. A drug empire? A sweatshop? Dog fights? Sex slaves?

My mind races, trying to fill in blanks I can hardly imagine, and I clutch the broken bits of plastic like they're a talisman against chaos. The jagged edges bite into my palm, but the pain keeps me focused. I squeeze harder and yelp when I break the skin.

Noah whirls around, eyes wide. "What's wrong?"

Stone pushes through the door, but I can't see past Noah's broad body.

"Nothing." I transfer the pieces to my other hand and hold up my palm to show him just how much nothing it is. Only a small cut. But he reacts like I've sliced off a finger. He knocks the rest of the phone to the ground, wraps a hand around my wrist, and pulls me close to study the wound.

"You hurt yourself." His eyes flash fire, and his voice is a clenched fist, seething and restrained.

I don't understand his response at all, but I need to. I need to understand the rules of his world, this dark realm. "You're angry?"

"Nobody hurts what's mine. Not even you."

The arrogance. I bristle. How can he possibly… "My body is still my own."

He pulls me closer and presses his mouth to the cut on my hand. With his head bent, the gesture is almost sweet, *kissing it better.* Then wet heat slicks across the scrape, sending shocks up my arm and straight down to my clit. It's lewd and filthy, and I never want him to stop.

"This is mine," he whispers against my skin, and then his other hand is between my legs, cupping my sex roughly. "This too, especially when we're on my bike or in this club, every inch of you belongs to me. Got it?"

He's squeezing me through my jeans while he runs his lips and tongue over my wrist like an animal marking its territory. I wonder if he'll mark me lower—use his mouth instead of his hand—out here in the empty parking lot. Then I wonder how long the parking lot *stays* empty, and my whole body flushes hot when I realize I don't care.

The pleasure is sharp—I'm still so sensitive it's almost painful—and then it stops. It takes me a second to realize he's waiting for an answer. "God, yes."

Of course *yes*. The only answer is *yes* out here in the middle of nowhere with a junkyard dog wandering the perimeter. Isn't it? I wonder what he'd do if I said no. Drive me back to the apartment I'm probably evicted from and dump me on the curb? Throw me over his shoulder and haul me into the club anyway? I flush even hotter because...*yes* to that too.

"Sweetheart, you keep calling me *God* like that and I'm gonna lose my mind. Probably do something stupid like fuck you when I'm supposed to be working. You're gonna get me killed

FOUR

Inside the club it's not the wall of noise and heat that buckles my knees. It's not the men with guns and the half-naked women. It's the smell. Smoke, sweat, stale beer, motor oil, and a hint of something sweet. A spritz of cheap perfume over the wreckage of a bender.

The signature scent of my childhood.

It wraps around me like an unwanted hug, dank and cloying. The memories are ashes in my mouth. A fist around my heart. They are a papery hand on my thigh and my eyes locked on a pineapple air freshener swinging from the cracked rearview mirror while I press my knees together so hard it leaves a bruise. *Aloha.*

I breathe in shallow pants, just like I did back then, trying not to fill my nose—my lungs—with the stink. I don't want it inside me. The smell is more of a wake-up call than a pot of coffee.

I hadn't escaped my old life. I'd endured it and crawled out of the rubble, clawing my way to a subsistence existence. For what? To walk into this pit a willing victim? Giving up every inch of ground I've managed to gain? For a thrill ride? For an orgasm or three? God, what the hell have I done?

Noah clamps his arm around my shoulders, holding me up and herding me along. "It looks worse than it is."

His touch grounds me in the present, pushing back some of that old panic. These are hands that have protected me and pleasured me, cleansed me and claimed me. My scalp tingles at the memory of his tender touch.

There are people everywhere. Crowding a make-shift bar, flanking a pool table. Laughing and shouting. Fucking and fighting. Two topless girls maneuver through the crowd, each with a tray of shots. Their denim cutoffs are so short the pockets hang below the frayed hems like little white flags. *Waitresses.* I wonder if they picked their uniforms. If they paid for them. Somehow I can't imagine these outlaws with their grizzled beards and

1% patches offering a 401k and clothing allowance. Shit, it's not like Jimmy does either.

I lean into him, drawing strength. "It looks like hell."

"You're a guest of the Devil's Host. Where else would I bring you?"

The demon patch I'd studied while riding behind Noah is everywhere. Goat horns, flaming eyes, a hollow skull. It stares at me from every broad back. It laughs at me from a banner over the bar. But this isn't hell. Hell is a pineapple air freshener and a roaming hand. Hell is an empty stomach and no food for days. Hell doesn't have music or cold beer or guys getting blow jobs in the corner while everyone else goes about their business.

A man hooks his arm out and snatches up one of the waitresses. The tray of shots crashes to the ground. Glass breaks like tinkling bells, adding another layer of grit and booze to the already sticky floor.

She squirms in his arms, but her laugh is so loud. "You greedy fucker. Now I'll have to clean that shit up."

She slaps him, and it's like slow motion—her small hand flying across his hard face. My stomach drops. I can't watch what happens next, but I can't look away. I brace for it.

The big man with greedy hands just smiles. "I'll have a prospect push a mop. You've got better things to do."

She climbs his body like a tree and kisses him like *she* owns *him*. Like it's her right.

I wonder if ownership works both ways. If the *owned* have their hooks in just as deep. I look up at Noah. "What would you do if I slapped you?"

His eyes narrow, and he pulls me tighter. "That depends on whether or not I deserve it."

"Is that how all this works, you get what you deserve?"

"No, baby. Here you get what you take and you keep what you can hold."

Two men approach us slow and steady. If the club is a lawless jungle, they are the big cats stalking in the darkness. One is broad and blunt, solid as his name. *Stone.* The other is lean and feral with a smile that never touches his dead eyes. He looks almost scrawny compared to Noah and Stone with their thick necks and thicker arms. But there's a fierceness in his features that tells me this is not a man to fuck with. The ink on his arms is all black and gray, subtle, spiderwebs and skulls and cold black stars. When he smiles at me, my skin crawls. Noah stiffens.

"The prodigal son returns. And he comes bearing gifts." Dev—it has to be Dev—takes my hand and brushes his lips over my knuckles. I jerk my hand back like he's touched me with a lit match. His dead eyes flicker. "Did you get lost on the way to grandmother's house? What's your name?"

A sinking feeling washes over me. I'd been outraged at the idea of fucking Noah as payment for Harry's debt and then intrigued. But right now I'm starting to think I might have to do more than just Noah.

"You don't need her name. She's a guest," Noah all but growls. "My guest."

Dev smirks and drops my hand. "I thought maybe this sweet piece was here for our tweaker friend. A little leverage. He's a *guest* too."

"Harry is here?" My heart races, and I instantly regret speaking at all. Noah hadn't even wanted to give Dev my name, but he seems to know who I am already.

"He's *hanging around* here somewhere." Dev turns back to Noah. "Let's give your guest a tour. I thought I was going to have to send you out to pick her up, looks like you were planning ahead." Dev turns back to me. "Come on, Star."

Yeah, he knows exactly who I am. Stone's eyes widen and Noah's mouth flattens into a thin, hard line. "We need to talk about some business, Dev. Luca's. Jimmy's. Shit is going sideways."

"Not in front of company."

I'm company. An outsider who already knows too much and now it's clear Dev knows that I know. Both Noah and Stone seem surprised by Dev's knowledge. Between this revelation and the stuff about Luca at the strip mall it's obvious that Dev is working some angle his men aren't aware of and wouldn't approve. But they're both cautious, calculating glances passing between them. When they fall into step behind Dev anyway, I don't have any choice but to follow the monster into his lair.

The tour is just a walk deeper into the warehouse. In a back room that might've been an office in another life, I see Harry strung up against a wall. Coarse rope wraps his wrists and pulls his arms high above his head. This exceeds my worst fear. "Oh God. Oh God. OhGodohGodohGod."

I cover my mouth because I can't seem to make myself stop crying out any other way. Red welts streak his bared chest, and his face is swollen. My eyes sting from the smoke and unshed tears. It's awful seeing him like this. Frail and exposed. Broken. But he'd taken their money and he'd run. Did he deserve this? No. I couldn't believe that. Nobody did.

Noah looks at Harry and looks at Dev. "You've been entertaining yourself."

His voice is so flat, like he's working very hard to keep it that way. I wonder if he thinks Harry deserves this. And I think maybe his answer is very different from mine.

Dev's lip curls into a sneer. "I had to do something when you weren't returning my calls."

Stone interrupts, and I'm reminded of the lengths he's gone to, to help Noah. To save him from Dev's wrath. "Smitty picked him up on the interstate. This shithead went on the run with an empty gas tank."

"This *shithead* won't tell me what I want to know. Maybe he will now that we've got her to persuade him." Dev picks up a branch leaning against the wall beside Harry, bends it and lets it snap back. It has to be what he's been using on Harry, a stick, a *switch*—and his fists. Harry and I both flinch.

Well, I flinch. Harry jerks against his bonds. "I swear to fucking Christ, Dev. Nobody else is moving product in your area. She don't know anything. I never took her on any runs."

"She's not here to answer questions. You'll be doing that. We know you like her. *Everyone* seems to like her." Dev's gaze flicks to Noah, and my whole body goes cold. Maybe I'm leverage for more than just Harry. Dev could use me to get to Noah too. "Unless you enjoy listening to a lady scream."

My heart hammers out of my chest, and I am falling. I see Noah wrestled back by three men in leather vests. I hear his roar. Then everything goes dark.

FIVE

"Shhh." Noah shushes me as I wake. He's all around me, the heat of him and the weight of his shadow. He holds me still with one hand around my throat, cupping my chin, and the other threaded through my fingers above my head. It's like the reverse of when a mama cat grabs a kitten by the scruff. I want to lean into that touch, use the weight of my body to show him how much harder I'd like it.

"Mmm," I whimper.

When I move my head, my brain sloshes a half a second behind the motion. A fog curls between my thoughts. It feels a little like that time I popped an Ambien from one of the girls at work and chased it down with half a beer. There's a sour taste in my mouth. *Bile.* I'm not just stilled by his touch. I'm pinned to the wall with the sick taste of fear still thick on my tongue. Topless.

Oh God.

My shoulders are on fire. I try rolling them to ease the ache, but I really can't move. My hands are trapped, bound above my head with more than just his grasp. My feet barely touch the floor. It's not Noah holding me up.

My eyes fly open, fear stripping away the last haze of sleep—or unconsciousness—and all I can see is Noah's face inches from mine. Panic rips through my body as I tug and jerk against the scratchy rope wrapped around my wrists. "What the f—"

Noah releases my neck and clamps his hand over my mouth.

"Shhh, shhh. Be still. You'll hurt yourself."

A terrible laugh catches at the back of my throat. I'm already hurt, hurting, will hurt again. Being still won't stop that. My breath puffs against his fingers in short pants; the fine hairs on his knuckles tickle my nose.

"You fainted. It's okay. I'm here. Shhh." Noah smooths my hair back as he shushes me. My heart slows, but my mind races. Noah is here. They didn't take him away. But nothing else about this situation is okay. His eyes are sad, almost pleading. "I shouldn't have— I'm sorry. It's better this way. I couldn't let Dev be the one to…"

He brushes his lips against my forehead in a trembling kiss. It hits me that he's scared too. Or worried at least. I hadn't thought he could be worried. Inconvenienced maybe. Or annoyed. Worry is frightening.

He steps back, dropping his head like he can't bear to look at me. I want to ask what he shouldn't have done, what he's sorry for, what's better, but all my words are twisted into a shriek when Dev steps out of the shadows and a sharp pain sears across my arm.

My whole world narrows down to a stinging strip of flesh and the gravel of their voices. "Enough with the tender-mercies bullshit. Unless you're going to fuck her for my amusement, get to work."

Heat spreads over my cheeks, and there's a sick churn in my belly. Embarrassment for a thing that I would have liked, turned twisted and cruel. I would have wanted Noah to fuck me for someone's amusement. Would have wanted him to take me rough against a wall. Just not *this* wall. Or for *this* man's amusement.

Dev. Scary, feral Dev. I shudder.

Noah snarls back at him. "This isn't work, you sick bastard. It's a carnival freak show. You want me to earn? Give me five minutes with Harry."

"You had a whole day. And all you did was chase some tail. Now you don't even want to share your toy. A few hours on her back can't buy what I'm after anyway."

Noah's gaze licks over me like brush fire, hot and possessive. He lunges at Dev, and three guys are on him in seconds. It takes all of them to hold him back. The muscles in his arms, the tendons in his neck bunch and flex with the strain. He'd been barely contained menace in the diner; now he's all checked fury and regret. "She's my responsibility. I brought her here. If something needs doing, I'll be the one doing it."

"Did you leave a little of your brain on the side of the highway somewhere? There's no if, Noah." Dev studies him with that calculating lizard glare of his, cold and heavy-lidded. I can see him searching for weak spots, taking Noah's measure and finding him lacking. "This is about loyalty. You seem to have lost that too. Maybe it's running down the inside of her thigh? We should check."

Noah jerks, and two more guys step out of the shadows. They stand like bookends beside Dev. Noah doesn't have anywhere to go but I get the feeling he'd be pacing like a caged tiger if he could move. One-on-one, Noah could break Dev over his knee, but fair fights aren't for outlaw bikers. Together, they could kill him. Tear him apart with their bare hands.

My mouth goes bone-dry. That's exactly what will happen. If Noah doesn't go along with whatever they want, they will kill him. And they'll kill me too.

"I'm loyal, but I didn't sign up for this."

"Enforcer. It's right there in your fucking title. *Force.* You signed up to hurt people. For the club."

Noah drops his chin to his chest and shakes his head. "Not women."

Dev laughs, and the sound is so shockingly out of sync with everything about him I break out in goose bumps. "Quit stalling, or I'm going to peel that patch off your body, shove it down your throat and make you watch while I—"

"I'll do it."

"I'm running out of patience. Make the bitch scream or I will. And I won't stop with her."

Dev's commands slice me deeper than the switch. Noah can be strung up here beside me, both of us victims of Dev's *tender mercies.*

Or Noah can hurt me.

I'd wanted Noah to hurt me anyway, to fuck me up and push pause on all my failed plans. The kind of hurts I'd imagined seem almost sweet now: teeth, nails, the bruising force of his cock, a dirty mouth to flay me open. All my dark secrets exposed and examined. I wanted his big hands collaring my neck, reminding me—no matter the darkness—how precious every breath can be. But we're not alone in my apartment anymore. We're deep in his world, and the rules keep changing. Or crystallizing. *You keep what you can hold.*

Noah can hold me with each flick of the switch. The sharp breath before every scream, immeasurably precious. He can keep me. Marked, owned, used…but alive.

It's only pain.

Noah squares his shoulders and white-knuckles the switch in his left hand, the hand inked with LOST.

I want to tell him that it's okay, that I can take it, that I'll pretend we're alone and I might even like it, but I don't think Dev would appreciate my willing participation.

A battle plays out on Noah's face; there's a hard beauty in it. Fear and frustration. Duty and desire. I remember the way he cupped my hand outside and gritted his teeth at the sight of my scratch. *Nobody hurts what's mine. Not even you.*

Not even him. I can see that in the set of his jaw and the way he still won't look at me.

I need him to look at me. I force my body to relax and put as much forgiveness into my voice as I can. "Noah, please."

I hope Dev thinks I'm pleading for my life. I guess in a way I am.

"You hear that, Harry? Your cousin begs so pretty. I hope you hold out for a little while. I want to watch her dance."

Noah lifts the switch.

Oh, the relief. That Dev is buying it. That Noah is going through with whatever terrible bargain he struck with himself to save me from Dev.

His eyes finally meet mine, and there's so much sorrow there it squeezes my heart. I'm the one tied to the wall, but he's bound more tightly than any ropes could manage.

There's more than just our lives and his loyalty to the club at stake here. He's going to give up a piece of his soul to do this.

"I told you to run, Star."

"I'm sorry." I say it again and again. Litany, benediction, prayer. I don't know. The closest I've been to church in years is when the Lutheran men's group says grace over their Sunday lunch. I *am* sorry. Not that I climbed onto the back of his bike, but that he's suffering. And I'm glad that he has more honor than he needs. More than enough for the both of us. Because I have none. I'll do anything to get us out of here.

And now so will he.

The first strike is tentative. A caress. But I cry out like he's branding me. I add *please* to the litany. "I'm sorry. I'm sorry. Please. I'm sorry."

I put on a show until Noah's mouth is a grim line and Dev's eyes shine overbright in the darkness. Until I don't have to pretend anymore, because Noah has found a rhythm, found the quiet place inside himself that lets him endure what needs to be done.

I know it well.

I'd thought my past was dragging me down, but it was all me. Unable and unwilling to let go until this moment. I brace for the burn. Nothing matters but now. The next fifteen minutes. And living to see the fifteen after that.

We're both in the quiet place together. Surviving.

We'll get out of here alive, but we won't be the same. I'll be whole, and Noah will be irrevocably broken.

He's not my self-destruct button. I'm his.

SIX

I go somewhere in my mind. A place with soft grass instead of corrugated metal, a place that smells like honeysuckle instead of dank sweat. I stay there for a long time. There's a green field beside a lake, and Noah is rising up out of the water naked. His body is beautiful, the hard planes covered with wildflower colors. The stars are out and the sun is shining and nothing hurts. He reaches for me again and again. When he does, I dance to music only we can hear.

The lake is my tears. The switch, cutting through the air, is our song.

My body is awkward, jerking and swaying in the darkness. Every sharp crack tries to pull me back to the present, forces me to pay attention. I squeeze my eyes shut so we can be alone in that place where pain is pleasure. Where everything he does to me feels good because he's the one doing it.

All my moans belong to him.

I don't know how many strikes it takes for Harry to cave—five lashes? Fifty? I just know that he does.

"The Bloody Jokers. They didn't give me a choice either." Harry cries.

The rival club name is strange and none of his sobbing confession makes sense to me, but Dev is satisfied. He leaves Harry in a heap on the floor and stalks over to us. Fresh adrenaline spikes my bloodstream, and my heart stutters back to a racing gallop. I try to slow my breathing, to hide my fear from this monster, but I can't. I feel my nostrils flaring, see Dev's satisfied smirk. His gaze rakes over me, and it's like salt in every wound. He's cold, assessing, and so fucking pleased with himself. I hold my cry in my throat, trap it there, because he wants it more than anything. He wants my anguish and the anguish it will cause Noah. I refuse to give that to him too.

Whatever he wants, I'm going to make him fight for it if I can.

He smiles. "You were a very good girl. The club owes you a favor."

There's a heat in that smile that makes my stomach turn even as I'm relieved that this nightmare is ending. Having Dev owe me anything feels wrong, dangerous in a way climbing onto the back of Noah's bike never did. I think maybe the only thing Dev owes people is terror and chaos. "Then let me go."

"That's not up to me, sweetheart. You're his problem. And if he's anything like me, after that performance you aren't going anywhere."

My mouth floods with saliva, and I want to spit right in Dev's smug face. I'm reminded of snakes that swallow their prey whole and then don't eat for a month. That's the look on Dev's face. Like he'll be digesting tonight's entertainment for a long time. I pray that I'm right, because if he touches me again, I'm pretty sure Noah will lose his mind and we'll all end up dead.

I don't know much, but everything I know so far tells me Noah is nothing like him. Beneath the rough exterior, Noah has honor and kindness. Dev has none.

Noah stands frozen in front of me, and I mentally cheer for him. He's not taking what is so obviously bait. He stays like that—eyes forward, fists clenched—until all of Dev's men file out the door. The last of them drag Harry from the room, like it's a dark parade and he's the banner stretched between them. Maybe that's exactly what it is.

I imagine there's still coleslaw clinging to the bottom of his boots. I imagine him singing like it's closing time. Is it still Harry? Or just a body?

As soon as the door closes behind them, Noah drops the switch and picks up some of the rope they'd cut away from Harry's body.

"You went too far, Dev. I think maybe you've been doing that a lot lately."

Smug, self-satisfied, Dev doesn't move. "Too far? I decide what's too far. I draw the damn line."

Noah shakes his head and coils rope around his hands. "I've seen power break a man before. I've seen it twist a man until all that's left is greed and hollow cruelty. You may get to draw the line, but it's my job to hold it. Now I'm going to do my job."

"Good."

And then that angry wall of muscle is in motion again. The tiger unleashed. The cage broken. Dev doesn't have five men at his side anymore. He realizes that far too late. I watch the understanding and surprise break over his face and then I watch his eyes bulge.

"I'm going to hold the fucking line to your throat and choke you with it."

SEVEN

"You killed him for me." My voice cracks. My throat is dry and aching from all the crying out I've done and also from holding back. Exhaustion sinks deep into my bones, and I can hardly hold my head up.

Noah flicks open a pocketknife and attacks the knot at my wrists. "I killed him for a lot of reasons. What he did to you—what he made me do to you—that was an act of war. He knew I'd claimed you, and he made me hurt you anyway. For the club. It's not supposed to be that way. Twisted like that. We may be criminals, but there's a code of fucking conduct. Unspoken. And spoken. This shit broke all of the rules. And those fuckers just stood by and let it happen. No, they helped him do it. I can't let it stand."

Those fuckers? He meant the other men in the room. The ones who grabbed him when I fell, the ones who made sure he did what needed to be done. Is he going after them now? My mind spins on war, though. They certainly have enough guns and men, but all of them against Noah? Is he as crazy as Dev?

The knot at my wrist gives, and I slump into Noah's arms.

Noah cradles me like a handful of broken glass swept off the floor—light and careful, like I might cut him or shatter further. I want his solid arms to squeeze me, to remind me that I am flesh and bone and pumping blood. I feel insubstantial, shivering and floating above the horror of this dark little room.

I worry that he feels insubstantial too.

"Hold me tighter." I ask because it will do us both good.

"It'll hurt."

"I don't care."

He gathers me close and traces the curves of my face with the rough edge of his thumb—over my nose, my cheeks, brushing my hair from my forehead. "You gotta start caring, Star. Because I'm caring too much right now. It's tearing me up inside how much I care."

I can hardly look at him. His touch and voice and eyes are all so soft right now it's almost scary. I knew what to do with his hardness, but this? His tenderness rains down on me like the sweetest hail. Pinging against my defenses.

"What about Harry? Where'd they take his...?" I can't bring myself to say the word body. ."

He traces soothing circles into my scalp. "You can't worry about that. He may not have chosen his life, but he chose his death. He knew the penalty for throwing in with the Bloody Jokers, the price of betrayal."

"And Kristi? Her shop?"

"I'll deal with it."

I curl my arm around his neck and press my face into his shoulder, hiding from betrayal and prices and everything awful. "Can't we just leave?"

He skims his hand over my back and upper arms. I wince when he hits a sore spot, but he doesn't stop touching. Jesus, he's not avoiding my injuries. He's checking me, methodically. "This is my whole life here. My brothers. My family. My job. I can't walk away and let them destroy it all unchecked."

I'd walked away from my whole life.

Twice.

That this one had such a hold on him, that he thought it was worth staying for—dying for—was confusing and intriguing. I wanted that for myself. "You have a family?"

Noah nods. "My old man had to quit riding a few years back. Got a sister too. Jules. She's nineteen and a handful." He presses a kiss to the corner of my lips that lights a fire inside me, inside both of us.

His hungry mouth claims mine, gentle at first but then fierce, until it's all wet heat and teeth.

His tongue slides against mine and his fingers dig into my ass while I'm cradled in his arms, and it's like I can finally breathe again. I'm not just a problem to be dealt with or collateral to be protected. I'm his. I'm wanted.

"I can't hurt you again. Not one fucking hair on your head."

For the first time in my life, in this horrible place, with this man who does horrible things, I feel cherished. "When you hurt me, it felt like love."

"That's fucked-up, Star. And it's why I need to get you the hell out of here. Get you safe."

"I don't want to be protected, though. Not like that. I want to be with you. Does what I want count at all?"

"No." Half growl, half smile—he nips my bottom lip, and another flood of warmth spreads through my body, chasing away the chill and fear. "What I just did? That was a bloody fucking coup. I have to deal with the aftermath, we don't have a chance in hell if I don't."

Hope swells in my chest. "But we do have a chance?"

"I guess we've got a chance. Maybe. If I survive the blood feud Dev started with the Jokers. If I survive cleaning up the mess he made of our club while I wasn't paying attention. If I survive the way my fucking cock gets hard every time you so much as blink in my direction. There's a lot of fucking ifs. Even then I still won't deserve you, but I'm a selfish fucker so I'll take you anyway. If."

All those ifs, and the only one I can think about is attached to his cock. It's the only one I can do anything about. "Is it hard now?"

"Are you blinking?"

"Fuck me, Noah." The request is a sigh, a plea, an involuntary response. Totally inappropriate, one hundred percent ridiculous, but I don't care. We might never have another chance. "If everything is about to go to shit, let's at least have that before it does. I want you inside me."

"Here?" He means this awful room where terrible things happened. To Harry. To me. To him.

"Make it go away. Make us both forget. For now."

He sets me down, and I wobble on my feet for the first time in what feels like hours. He shoves a wooden chair under the doorknob, and then I'm spinning. My hands are against the wall, and Noah is behind me, yanking down my jeans. Two tugs and my ass is bare. His belt buckle clinks, and I know his jeans are down too. The crinkle of a wrapper. His sharp inhale as he rolls on a condom.

My body melts, sore and tired but wound so damn tight waiting for him to touch me. He gathers my hair into his fist and presses a kiss to the back of my neck. "This is what you want?"

"Yes," I hiss as his other hand slips down the front of my body, pinching my nipples, teasing my belly, then finally dipping between my legs to torment my clit. Fast. Hard. Painful. It's what I want. What I need. Especially after all that slow torture. I need it to burn.

"If I were a good man, I wouldn't do this."

I'm so wet, but there's no embarrassment in this moment. Not after all we've done tonight. "Would a good man touch my pussy like that, feel how ready I am, and walk away? No. You're good, Noah; I know you are."

He whips me around to face him. There's nothing soft in his eyes now, only violence and hard lust. I reach for him, and he lifts me up. Finally, finally his cock is at my entrance, the blunt head spreading me open, filling me up.

Noah is holding me in his arms so tight and filling me so full. Our eyes are locked, dark with something more than lust. We are needful in this moment. We need each other. I'm soft where he is hard. Light where he is dark. I'm not broken glass. I'm unbreakable. I bend and bend. I take everything he gives me, every angry thrust, and shudder around him.

Claimed and claiming.

The orgasm rips through us both like a battle cry.

EIGHT

I wake up in Noah's room at the club for the second day in a row, and my first thought is the same one I've had each time—it's nicer than my apartment.

Not because it's clean—it really isn't. Or because of the fancy amenities—it has none. But because every inch of the space is so unapologetically his.

My memories from a few nights before cut through the haze of sleep. The beating. The bodies. Noah hauling me in here for the first time, tossed over his shoulder—broken, sore, terrified—with the hoots and wolf whistles from his brothers still ringing in my ears. He must have looked like a conquering Viking to them. That would make me the spoils of a war they didn't even know happened, except for the few who'd been blindly loyal to Dev. *God, were they all dead now too? Had Noah and Stone torn through them all yet?* Then I'd wept tears of relief as soon as we crossed the threshold because I'd felt so deeply that this room was an inner sanctum, safer somehow than anywhere else in the club, a place where only Noah could touch me.

He'd touched me so gently. He'd fucked me hard in that awful place, but here everything had been soft. He'd undressed me. Smoothed something cool and slick over my welts. Whispered apologies into my skin. Ordered me to sleep.

And that's what I'd done. For days.

Now, I'm awake. Rested and alert. Hyperaware. Taking it all in again.

His walls are covered with a kind of collage. Bikes and centerfolds and whiskey-ad sunsets. I can almost picture him thumbing through the pages of a parts catalog or a dirty magazine, coming across some shiny thing he wants for himself, and tearing it out to feather his nest. Building the life he wants layer by layer. I want to touch each one and ask him for the story that goes along with it. Because they *are* all stories. I know that much. It's not wallpaper; it's a vision board. And I'm the latest addition.

I'm on my side, pinned by the force of Noah's will and the weight of his body. He's spooned behind me. Clinging to me, really. He's got one arm under me, hooked up so his massive palm crushes my breast. The other arm is draped over my waist—that palm cups my pussy. Every breath I take shifts my body just enough to rub my most tender places against his callused fingers. My nipples are already hardening, the bundle of nerves near the top of my mound plumping and tightening.

I don't want to be turned on like this, so easily. It's embarrassing. He's going to wake up with my wetness coating his hand. My cheeks burn, remembering what he did the last time. The way he'd shoved his fingers into my mouth so I could clean them. Lick them like a cock, his cock, the one that is hard and hot against my back.

I rock my hips.

He makes a sleepy noise, half grunt, half moan, and then he's rocking with me. He traps my nipple between two fingers and rolls it, sending sharp shocks of pleasure spearing from my breast down to my clit. "Greedy girl."

"I am." I whine. I don't want to do that either, but I can't help it. Every stroke and flick makes me so needy and desperate. I'll do almost anything, suffer almost any indignity just to have this. To have his mouth on me, his cock inside me.

I've already suffered so much it should be my reward.

"Take what you want, Star. If you're going to survive in this place, you're gonna have to learn."

I turn to do just that, but he flexes his muscles and clamps me in place. "Hey, I can't move."

"I didn't say it'd be easy."

"Don't you want—"

"Feeling you struggle in my arms has my dick so fucking hard right now, baby."

Oh shit. I don't know if it's a game or a lesson or both, but everything that had been a sleepy simmer is suddenly at a raging boil. I'm small and naked, and his hand is wrapped around my throat. I can't do what he's asking me to do. It goes against my every instinct.

I whimper, and he growls in response, squeezing me tighter. "Fight me."

Do I have any fight left in me? With his palm caressing my windpipe and his leg wrapped over mine?

I can breathe—just. His grip is solid, restrictive and restrained, an undeniable reminder that he is powerful, that his body is a weapon with the safety on. And then I *can't* breathe when he clamps down harder. Just for a second. Just long enough for my vision to go hazy at the edges. Adrenaline jolts through me, tightening every muscle, raising every hair. My heart is a hummingbird in a steel cage beating out *yes yes yes* with its wings.

Yes. I can fight.

Hemmed in, I can't really use my fists or my feet. I can hardly move. But I can dig my nails into the hand at my throat. I can slam my elbow into his ribs.

So I do.

I yank and tug and writhe until I'm covered in a sheen of sweat from the exertion. His cock only seems to get hotter and harder at my back. A thick promise, taunting me. Maybe if I had a pry bar, I could get him off my neck. Get some leverage. My ragged nails don't do more than scrape off a layer of his skin. He grunts at the blows to his gut though and works the fingers on his other hand between the lips of my pussy.

Finally.

It's a cruel touch, blunt and rough. But my body is already melted for him. It gives way, easy and slick, so he skates over my clit. My hips buck, eager to take what he'll give me. To take what I want.

He laughs. "Fight harder. A few little love taps aren't going to get you anywhere."

"Got you touching my clit," I pant, still clawing the hand at my throat.

"But you want more than that. You're so empty and aching, I can feel it." He thrusts two fingers inside me, and I clench around him as he pumps in and out. He uses quick, shallow thrusts that only make me more desperate for something deeper, harder, faster. "I could play like this for days. Getting you close but never all the way. Getting my hand all messy so you can clean it for me. Is this what you wanted? My fingers inside your hot cunt again."

He is infuriating. As relentless and unchangeable as the tide. As immovable as a mountain.

I grit my teeth. "You know what I want."

"You want them in your tight little asshole then?"

I hadn't even thought of that. My mind screams *no no no,* but my pussy gushes around his fingers because *please please.* And still he strokes, the wet noises drowned out by my whimpers.

I shake my head, unable to give voice to this conflicted desire. I want him filling me up…everywhere. Too much and not enough. Deep and hard. Soft and slow. The teasing, the torment, it's nearly unbearable. I just want him to fuck me again. To claim me in the daylight. To take me as a woman, not as a debt to be collected or a prize to be won or a victim to be soothed.

"I don't want your fingers. I want your cock." All that wanting builds and builds without anywhere to go. I'm frantic with need, frustrated, almost angry with it. If I could bite him, I would. "Pin me to your fucking wall and make me come already."

His grip loosens around my neck, and then we're rolling until he's on top of me. "You don't go on my wall. My wall is for shit I'll never have, places I'll never go. I'll fuck you in my bed where you belong."

The mattress bounces as he springs up, and I'm so close I nearly come from the subtle vibration. Or from his declaration. I can't even process that right now. It's probably meaningless. One of those things people say in the throes of passion. Oh God.

He grabs a condom off his nightstand and rolls it on, looming over me like a dark angel with his lips curled into a victorious sneer. Because I fought him? Because he can have me? Both?

I slip a hand between my legs to tease him a little, to give him a show. But as soon as my fingers brush that needy throbbing, I'm lost. Skimming and pressing and skimming again. It's all for me.

Take what you want.

THE DEVIL'S HOST MC

His hands are hot on my ass, lifting me up and then finally, finally, finally plunging deep into my pussy. Filling me in a way his fingers never could. I grab the back of his head and pull him down for a kiss that turns feral. Tongues and teeth. More taking. We are a clash of bodies, fighting for the same peak.

When we come, it's like the world is ending. Maybe it is.

The sound of the headboard banging against the wall is replaced by another banging. The thump of fist against wood.

And then Stone is standing at the foot of the bed. Noah doesn't get up. He just yells over his shoulder while his cock softens inside me. "I'm getting tired of this shit, brother. You want in this bed, you're gonna hafta buy me dinner first."

"It's Jules."

Jules, that's the sister he mentioned the other night. The handful. Noah stiffens at the sound of her name. "What's she done now?"

"You should get dressed. We can talk then." Stone's voice is tight with worry.

"Is my bare ass making you uncomfortable? Just spit it out."

"Your dad found an ace of diamonds in her bed. She's gone, Noah. The Bloody Jokers have her.

DRIVE ME WILD

PART 3 OF 4

ONE

The longer I wait for someone to come get me, the harder it is to stay still. For the first fifteen minutes after Noah left to meet with the other club officers, I sat quietly and focused on the weave pattern in the thermal blanket spread over his bed. For the second fifteen minutes, I traced my finger over the curves of every pin up model gracing his walls. His commitment to diversity is impressive. His appreciation for a phenomenal rack, unquestionable. Now I am aggressively folding laundry— anything to keep my hands busy. I assume the clothes are clean. Dark t-shirts, jeans, bandanas and soft flannels. The earthy scent of him lingers in the laundry just beneath the mountain spring blast of detergent freshness. I only press my face into it twice. Okay, three times.

I only wonder who washes it for him once.

I pull the t-shirt away from my face and fold it again.

There's a gentle rap on the door and then it creaks open. A young guy with barely more than a milk mustache on his upper lip pokes his head inside Noah's room. If we were back at the diner I might joke with him about his baby face, ask him if he wanted crayons while he waited for his eggs and bacon. Instead he's here to take me on a gallows walk. "They're ready for you now."

I want to ask him what's happened so far or if he's heard any news about Noah's sister. I want so many things but instead I drop the t-shirt I've been folding and smooth my skirt.

Deep breath, Star. Deep breath.

Noah promised me before he left for this meeting that even if they decided the worst, I'd still be okay because he and Stone had cleared out the club's cancer. That's what he'd called Dev and his men. A cancer.

I just hope the club stays in remission. I didn't ask what the worst might be.

The kid escorting me is a prospect. I know this because it's emblazoned on his back and because Noah explained a little bit about how the club works. His version of pillow talk. Now I know there are prospects, guys who want to be members and are on a kind of indefinite trial run until they prove themselves. Then they become full members. And I know there are rules and by-laws.

Noah broke them when he killed Dev without a vote.

I swallow hard as we pass the room where it all happened. It feels like a lifetime ago, but it was only a few days.

The rumble of voices drifts into the hallway from behind another door, and the prospect stops in front of it. He knocks more forcefully than he did for me, but he looks grimmer. Oh. He's hiding his nerves behind a rough expression. A little boy, determined not to be afraid of the dark.

I want to give him a snack and a juice box and tell him that it's almost never the dark you need to be afraid of; the things that come for you in the daylight are so much worse.

He opens the door, wraps his fingers around my upper arm and pulls me inside. Sunlight filters through the blinds in sharp slants, highlighting dust motes and smoke curls, casting shadows on the grizzled faces gathered around the long conference table. There are a dozen of them at least.

Hard, angry faces. With heavy brows and unruly beards. My heart hammers into my breastbone like it might escape this inquisition, and I search for Noah in the lineup of intimidation.

Noah sits in the corner, back to the wall, with a full view of the whole room. His eyes rake over my face and body, dark and possessive, communicating more than I can follow in a few seconds. Reassurance, sorrow, desire. Anger at the sight of the prospect handling me. Hope.

Stone sits beside him, equally tense.

I don't recognize anyone else at the table except for the big man who'd gotten his face slapped the night I arrived. When he opens his mouth to speak first, relief washes over me. At least I've witnessed his kindness.

"Honey, I'm Zig. I'm going to ask you some questions and you're going to tell us the truth. You do that and nothing bad happens. Got it?"

I nod.

"Did Noah promise you protection when he brought you here?"

Protection. What does that even mean? My knees start to buckle, and I'm grateful for the prospect's grip. He was going to make me fuck off Harry's debt, that didn't seem very protective. Except every other thing about him was hyper-protective. I was his, he'd reminded me of that over and over. I guess protection meant different things to different people. I'd let them decide. "He said I'd be working off my cousin's debt in trade, but if I did what he told me I wouldn't be hurt."

"Was the trade specified?"

This sounds like something from a legal contract. Jesus, I hadn't realized bikers were freaking lawyers or something. It makes sense though, criminals would be intimately familiar with the law. What do they call them on TV? Jailhouse lawyers. And the way they sit around staring at me, weighing my words, they're also jury and judge.

And executioners. I gulp. *Just tell the truth.* "Sex."

There's muttering and nodding. Zig takes a long drag from his cigarette and crushes it in a plastic ashtray shaped like a skull. "How were you hurt?"

Not just *were you hurt* but *how.* They've already discussed this. Determined I'd been hurt. I'm not here to tell my story, I'm here to corroborate or clarify. I'm here to protect Noah. Or damn him.

Are these the type of men who go soft inside at the first trickle of a woman's tears—or are they the kind who get angry? I have no way of knowing so I mimic the men at the table, the prospect beside me, and make my voice as flat as possible. Make my face stony. These are facts. Hard and true. Unemotional. "Dev made Noah beat me—torture me—to get information from my cousin. I'm certain if Noah had refused, he would've killed him. And me."

"Bullshit." A weathered man with wild dark hair and full beard slams his fist on the table. "There were five other men in that room. Two of them full members. And not one of them spoke up? You're a lying little whore."

Noah is up and out of his seat before I can blink, his palms flat on the table and his eyes flashing fire as he leans over, yelling. "You should apologize for that, Dale."

Dale sneers. "You brought her here to whore for a debt and you want me to apologize for calling her one?"

"I want you to apologize for calling her a liar. Whore is a fucking compliment. The whores bring more money into this club than anything you do. Now can we get this over with because in case you bastards have forgotten, my sister is missing. So vote to kill me and Stone and go look for her. Or vote *not* to kill us so *I* can go look for her."

Terror rips the words from my throat. "Kill you?" It's more of a shriek than a question. I hadn't thought they'd kill him. Me, maybe. But I thought the ones who'd wanted him dead were already taken care of. That's what he'd told me, they'd destroyed the cancer. God, what had I thought they were going to do? Give him detention? How could I still be so naïve—so stupid—given everything I've seen, everything I've done, and everything I've had done to me?

Nobody pays attention to my question.

Zig bangs his ashtray. "We haven't forgotten your sister. She's the reason we're having this meeting now instead of tonight at our normal time. Half the guys here are voting proxies for Devils who are still on the road. I'm sure they'd like to vote their own piece, but this is an emergency. We're not monsters."

Dale spits into a soda bottle filled with a brown liquid. My stomach lurches as I remember that sickly sweet smell. The buzz of a fly thumping inside a bottle, trapped, poisoned, dying. The foul taste of tobacco juice left behind on my lips no matter how furiously I rubbed away the unwanted goodnight kisses. The awful memory is so distracting I have to struggle to pay attention when Dale speaks. "You assassinated our fucking president, Noah. You and your boy murdered two other members—one of them my goddamn blood brother—and three friends of the club. There's a pile of fucking bodies with your names on them and there will be hell to pay. I don't care who your daddy is, who took your sister." Dale spits again and stares right at me. "Or who made any fucking promises to some lying truck stop skank."

SHARI SLADE

I shrug out of the prospect's hold and draw my shoulders back. "I am not a liar."

Stone pulls Noah back before he can launch himself completely across the table at Dale. "Now is not the time, brother." He keeps a hand on Noah's shoulder and looks to the man who's been questioning me. "Zig, are you done with her?"

Zig lights another cigarette, pulling so hard the cherry glows bright red even in the daylight, and blows out a billowing cloud of smoke. His eyes are bloodshot, and for one second I see exhaustion flicker across his face. "Yeah, you two take her and go wait in the bar. We'll let you know when we've made our decision."

TWO

Noah paces the length of the bar like a caged panther. I watch him in the cracked mirror that hangs on the wall behind the assorted bottles. He doesn't look worried or afraid. He looks like a predator, barely restrained. Deadly and silent. He hasn't said a word since he and Stone hustled me out of the club meeting. I can't blame him. Not with his fate undecided and his sister missing. Likely abducted by the same MC that got Harry in trouble—that got him killed.

A nervous giggle bubbles up and I choke it back. I don't know if I'm a captive or a guest. A victim or an ally. I was beaten and my cousin was killed. This is all so absurd.

I can't just sit here and wait for something to happen.

The scent of cooking bacon cuts through the beer-soaked ashtray smell clinging to every nearby surface. It practically pulls me out of my seat and lures me toward the kitchenette just off the side of the bar. I don't even realize I'm moving until Noah's hand is wrapped around my arm, pulling me back. "Where do you think you're going?"

"Someone's cooking breakfast. I don't know anything about what you do here, but I know how to crack eggs and deliver plates. I'll help." My stomach growls and the thin hard line of Noah's mouth quirks into a smile for half a second.

"And because you're hungry."

Embarrassed, I drop my gaze to study the tops of his boots. "I could eat."

His touch is gentle against my cheek, coaxing me with a crooked finger to look up at him. "I haven't been doing a very good job of taking care of you."

Then I see it—the anxiety in his eyes, the fear. The emotions he can't let anyone else see. It's exhausting keeping all that contained. I know firsthand. "You've had a lot going on."

"Don't make excuses for me, Star. I promised I'd do my best to keep you safe, to take care of you, and I've done nothing but fail you so far. I promised my sister I'd keep her safe too. Shit." He presses the heels of his palms into his eyes. "If you're hungry, I will fucking feed you."

He guides me to my stool, and moments later he's back with a plate of fluffy scrambled eggs, thick slices of bacon, and dark toasted bread. A pat of butter melts into the mountain of toast and I nearly weep at the sight. "This looks delicious. Thank you."

"It'll get the job done." He holds out a fork but when I reach for it he pulls it back, plunges it into the buttery eggs that have my mouth watering. My tummy rumbles again. Impatient. Painfully empty. But he doesn't steal my food, he lifts the loaded fork to my mouth and gently nudges my lips until they open.

Oh God. He's actually feeding me. Out here. In front of everyone. I swallow the bite and hardly taste it. My cheeks are on fire.

He spears some bacon. Delicious, smoky, salty, crisp. All the adjectives run through my mind as I moan my pleasure. I'm glad he's feeding me because if I had the fork I'd be gobbling it all down without taking a second to breathe. Noah forces me to go slow. To savor.

Sunlight washes into the room through the swinging front door, and Noah sets the fork down. An older man strides toward the bar. Two guys peel out of the shadows as if summoned by the invasion. Noah waves them off and meets the man halfway with a one-armed hug. "Pop."

His father stiffens and then melts into the embrace. "She didn't make a sound. I'd have heard her, she's a fighter. You know that."

"I know, Pop. Sit down. Eat something. I've got some calls out. We need information before we do anything." Noah settles him in the seat beside me and snaps at the girl with her head poked out of the kitchen. "Drew, bring another plate."

Drew bobs her dark ponytail at us and darts back to the grill. When she turns around I see she's wearing the same short-shorts under her apron as the shot girls were wearing at the club party the other night. My denim skirt hits the middle of my thigh and feels almost puritanical compared to the butt-bearing hem-line currently on display.

Noah's father has his arm slung over Noah's shoulders, taking comfort and support. It's almost strange to see the easy affection between them. I know they're family, but that closeness is so far outside my experience as to seem alien. The older man clears his throat. "Drugged. It's the only thing that makes sense. They came into my home and drugged my little girl. I want to paint the walls with their blood."

"We'll find her and we'll make them pay, but let's not talk business out here." They both look at me and it's startling how similar their features are. Noah's jawline is stronger, his nose sharper. But their eyes are almost exactly the same. It's like looking into Noah's future and seeing what he'll look like at 60. Or maybe it's like looking into Pop's past. "This is my…"

I want him to finish the sentence. I'm his what? His prisoner? His conquest? His?

He starts again. "My—"

"Pussy got your tongue? Jesus, son. Now isn't the time. I'm sure you're a real sweet"—Pop looks me up and down and his efficient inspection leaves me feeling stripped naked. Not in the good way— "girl, but we've got family matters to attend to right now."

Stone snorts and mutters something under his breath.

Drew sets a plate in front of Pop and picks mine up. She touches my arm and urges me along. "Come on back and help me with some dishes."

We stand side by side at the sink. I'm up to my elbows in soapy water and she's working a bar towel over a pint glass. I'm not surprised they sent me away or that Noah's father thought the worst of me. And I'm glad to have something to do, even if it is just washing dishes. I rinse another cup and hand it to Drew.

I'm not hurt that Noah didn't finish introducing me.

Not hurt much, anyway. But I keep my chin up and my spine straight. I rinse a handful of forks and pass them to Drew too. I'm alive. I've survived this long and I'm not about to stop now. I need to be thankful for that.

A stray curl escapes Drew's ponytail, and she tucks it behind her ear the way some people swat flies—a quick, unconscious movement. With the dart of her hand, order is restored. "For what it's worth, if you were just a piece of ass they wouldn't have acknowledged you at all. Don't feel sorry for yourself."

"I wasn't—"

"Sure you weren't." She shakes her head. Her tone is wry and almost wistful. And she doesn't look at me when she speaks. "I'm just like you, baby girl. Trying to find my way. My place. A word of advice? Never forget there's always someone coming up behind you. There's always someone who wants what you have, even when you think you've got nothing."

I'd never forget that. I've been the one *coming up from behind* my whole life.

It's hard to imagine I'm suddenly the one with something anyone wants, until I see Noah staring at me from the bar.

I have him. For now.

THREE

Zig and the other men from the meeting file out into the bar and I freeze. They were in that room alone, deciding Noah's fate, for a long time. Long enough for me to have breakfast and to wash possibly every single glass in the whole club. Long enough to come to terms with killing two men. My mind spins with possibilities I can barely imagine. At least they didn't come out with guns drawn, at least—

Drew slaps my ass. "Get it in gear, baby girl. We've got some filthy mouths to feed."

A sense of dread and a slap on the ass is basically how I've started every breakfast shift ever, so it isn't too difficult to shift into work mode. "What should I do? Scramble? Home fries?" I hold my hand a few inches from the grill to check the temperature.

Drew runs me off, smiling. "Get the hell away from that cooktop. This is my kitchen. You can prep plates and make toast."

I can't help but grin back, despite my fear for Noah and worry for Jules. There's work to be done. Work I know how to do. And Drew is as possessive and cranky as any short order cook I've ever encountered. Like Harry had been on his better days. A sadness pings my heart.

She sets a big metal bowl into the crook of her arm and whisks the heck out of a mess of eggs. I want to ask her if all she does for the club is cook, but that seems too forward. Even if she did just touch me inappropriately. I fill the eight-slice toaster with white bread and push down on the lever. "How many do you need?"

She scans the crowd filling up the bar. "Gimme twelve plates. Half white and half rye. One with an English muffin. They're hidden on top of the freezer." She spreads out two pounds of bacon slices. "Oh, but no butter on that muffin. He loves grape jelly."

"Who gets the love muffin?"

"God, don't let Zig hear you call it that." When she blushes I realize she's the girl I'd seen slapping the bearded mountain of a man the other night. And kissing him. "He may be a big old teddy bear once I get something sweet inside him, but—"

A bark of laughter cuts her off. Zig takes up the whole door frame. "I can think of something real sweet I want inside me right now."

"Unless it's preserves, you're out of luck."

"We can call your fine pussy juice preserves if you want. I could wipe it off my chin and spread it on my toast."

My face flushes about three shades darker than Drew's, and I try to disappear into the floor tiles. It doesn't work. Drew elbows me in the ribs. "I told you they had filthy mouths. But you knew that already, didn't you? And you—" she points her spatula at Zig "—you know you get an English muffin. Not toast."

"That's my good girl. Now hurry up, we need to feed everyone and then head up to the safe house. Looks like the Jokers took Jules last night."

"Fuck. I was hoping she'd just snuck out again."

"Am I gonna have time to pick up Ashlynn?"

"I already sent a prospect to pick her up from the sitter."

"Thanks, Zig. Is this all fallout from the change in leadership?"

Zig's eyes narrow, all the flirtatious twinkle gone. "Not your business."

Drew's lips go tight. She doesn't turn around as he walks away. Instead she flips the bacon and pours egg onto the hot griddle, then attacks it with a pair of spatulas.

"Is Zig your...old man?" The title feels wrong in my mouth, even though my mother had called enough of her boyfriends *old man* for it to seem normal. I don't think it meant the same thing to her as it does here.

"No. He likes me all right, and puts up with my shit, but I got a kid." She lowers her voice to a conspiratorial whisper. "I'm pretty sure that scares him to death."

"I'm sorry."

"That I have a kid? Don't be. Ashlynn is a damn angel. That little snot machine saved my life. The only reason I've got my shit together is for her."

It's not hard to picture Drew with a baby on her hip. Efficient, organized, determined. Sweet. I wonder what she'd been like before she got her shit together. "No, 1 meant about Zig. I'm sorry it won't work out with him. That's a shitty reason." And maybe not a real one considering Zig knew who the sitter was and made arrangements to have the little girl picked up.

"It's okay. It's good to know how the world works. He'll hook up with some sweet young thing with a lot less baggage, and I'll enjoy the ride in the meantime."

I think maybe the ride will last longer than Drew imagines. I wonder if Zig would come in here and flirt with Drew if he'd just delivered a death warrant to the men outside. I need to see Noah, right now. "Can I start delivering plates?"

"Yeah, stack 'em three deep on your arm if you know how. If not, I'll dig up a tray somewhere. I'll take Zig's."

"I can do it," I assure her, and start lining up plates. I leave the love muffin on the counter and try to imagine what it would be like to know something as innocent as how Noah likes his bread buttered.

The men don't look at me as I pass out plates, they just grunt "white" or "rye" as I pass by them. It takes me two trips to get them all out. And two more trips to deliver ketchup, hot sauce and pepper. Drew works behind the bar pouring tomato juice into glasses of beer while I make the rounds with a pot of coffee. Aside from the Red Eye cocktails, it's still not that different from Jimmy's. Hell, even the Red Eyes were popular with the kitchen staff. They just weren't on the menu.

I still don't know what's happening with Noah and Stone. None of the men are talking while they eat—there's no indication that I can read, no change in expression, no current of relief or renewed fear.

Finally, Noah reaches behind the bar and grabs a mug. I have an excuse to stand in front of him and hope he fills me in while I fill him up. Our eyes lock, and he says nothing as I pour. A nothing so loud my hands shake and coffee flows over the lip of the mug, onto Noah's hand and down the leg of his pants.

"Fuck, that's hot."

"Shit. Sorry. Sorry. Sorry." I flinch, half anticipating a blow for being stupid and wasteful. A reflex I can't seem to lose, no matter how many miles and years I put between myself and my childhood. My eyes fill with tears, more from stress and embarrassment than any real worry that I've hurt him. The coffee's been off the burner long enough it won't blister his callused skin. I fight the tears back.

He grabs the carafe from my hand and sets it on the bar. "It's okay, baby. We'll just clean it up."

He leads me out of the bar and back to his room. Once again, crossing that threshold sets me at ease. I feel safest in Noah's domain. "I'm so sorry I burned you. My brain was spinning with so many questions I couldn't pay attention to one more thing. What happened? How did they vote?"

He pulls me into his massive arms and smooths back my hair. *This is a hug.* Noah is hugging me and I never want it to stop. He presses a kiss to the top of my head. "They tabled the decision until after we find Jules."

"They decided...not to decide anything? They can't do that."

"They can and they did. It's good. It gives me and Stone more time to gather support. And it means we can start looking for Jules sooner."

"Has anyone called the police?"

"We take care of our own business."

"But it's your sister, if—"

"If I thought for half a second the cops could do a better job of finding Jules, I'd be the first to dial 9-1-1."

My pulse races erratic, stuttering and slamming so hard I can hardly get the words out past it. "Was it my fault they couldn't decide? Did I say the wrong thing?"

"No, baby. You did good. I was so damn proud of how brave you were."

His praise warms me from the inside out. I practically glow with it. I press my face into his shoulder. "Almost cried when Zig asked me how I was hurt. Almost cried again when I burned you."

"Almost." He pets my hair, stroking down my neck and over my shoulders again and again. "We're alone now, Star. Do you need to cry?"

As he asks me, his petting turns into something more. It's stroking. And then it's fingers tangling in my hair, pulling, yanking my head back. Tingles spread over my scalp and straight to my nipples. My eyes water. I yelp. Surprised and pleased. Confused. "Do we have time?"

"For me to give you something to cry about? I think so."

"Ok." He bends me over and pushes my face into the bedspread. The thermal weave I'd studied so closely is rough against my cheek. He holds me there with just the weight of his hand fisted in my hair.

"I'm going to spank your ass until it's all pink and perfect. Until your pussy is soaking wet and you're sobbing from it. Until you're wild and raw." He yanks my skirt up and my panties down in two brisk tugs. "And you're going to tell me when you've had enough crying, understand?"

I nod, the slight movement jerking at my scalp, sending a fresh wash of pleasure down my spine.

"And if you're really ruined—if your eyes are puffy and your face is swollen, if you're fucking wrecked, just the way I like—I'll lick your pussy until you come so hard on my tongue we both see

147

stars. You can do that for me, baby. Can't you? Let yourself go like that?"

Tears are already leaking from the corners of my eyes. Relief. I shudder with it. "Yes."

The bed creaks as he settles beside me and then the first crack of palm to ass vibrates through my body. It's a sharp heat and then it fades. A second crack, lower this time. A third, to the left. They layer together until my ass is all stinging heat and throbbing. I'm crying in earnest now. From the sharpness of the pain, the sweetness of the ache.

He spanks me again and again. On the end of every blow is a reverb that shoots straight to my clit, the pleasure on the other side of torment. I can feel moisture gathering between my lips every time I squirm and sob into the bedspread.

Everything feels swollen and ready. My pussy, my ass, my clit. God, my clit feels so hard I might come just from this. And I cry some more at the thought of not having Noah's tongue. I'm crying for orgasms I'll have and orgasms I won't. I'm crying just for the sake of crying and it feels amazing. I'm nothing but feelings, dancing on the edge of Noah's touch. Tender and brutal.

"I'm ruined." I cry out. But I'm not. Not nearly. I've got miles to go before Noah ruins me fully, drives me completely wild, wrecks me. I don't know if we'll have enough time together to get that far, but I'm ruined enough to make him happy in this moment.

He releases my hair. "Let me see."

I roll over, wincing when my sore bottom lands against the bed, and he sucks in a ragged breath. I can only imagine how I look, but if I were to guess based on his expression alone, I'd think I was more beautiful than I'd ever been. He kisses my eyelids, my cheeks, my lips. "So proud," he whispers.

He pushes my shirt up and kisses the tops of my breasts. He yanks at my bra cups until my nipples are exposed and kisses them too. Licks them until they're hard and aching. I squirm, jerking my hips up. Asking with my body for what he promised me. My reward. He kisses down my belly, darting his tongue around my navel, teasing.

And then he's kneeling at the edge of the bed, forcing my legs over his shoulders. There's no more teasing. Just more torment. His hot breath panting against the lips of my sex, a caress of its own. The swipe of his tongue. Once, twice, three times. Flicking the edge of that desperate bundle of nerves and opening my folds more with every pass. Slow and decadent. Electric. His hand flattens my belly, pulling me tight, opening me further. I watch him lap at me, his tongue curled, rolling against my clit until I'm bucking and squeezing his head with my thighs. Every movement spears fresh heat across my ass and adds to the fire Noah's stoking with every swirl and nibble.

He slips three fingers inside me, easy as anything, and stokes the fire from the inside too. I'm so wet and ready. The curve of his fingers, the stroke, drives me closer to the edge. Drives me over it, until I'm less than human. Until I'm nothing but blind need and hunger and *yes God yes*. He sucks and flicks and drags his teeth over my clit until I do see stars. Until there's nothing in the universe but my pussy and Noah's mouth and the supernova we make together.

I cry again. I sob while he kisses my thighs, my belly, my breasts, my lips, my eyelids. I weep while he loves my body back into existence.

His gentle touch is more brutal than any whip. He lashes me with everything I cannot have. *Forever* and *always* are things he's not built for. He's told me as much. It's not love. It can't be love. Not after everything we've been through. I remind myself of that over and over while my body trembles with the aftershocks.

FOUR

Noah's rough fingers are threaded through mine as he leads me up a tidy brick walkway. He holds my hand tightly, as if he can protect me with just his touch. But I can't figure out what I need protecting from in this suburban utopia.

It doesn't matter, I don't need to know a danger to brace for it.

I spot a tire swing swaying from a tree branch in the side yard and dusty pink roses climbing a trellis beside the porch. "Is this where you grew up?"

The lawn on either side of the brick walkway is storybook green and dotted with purple clover. A little unruly without edging into overgrown. Somebody cares about this lawn. Somebody cares about the house at the end of the walk, with its freshly painted shutters and gingerbread trim.

The front door is a cheery red. Bright. Shiny. The color of a drop of blood on the tip of a spindle.

"Yeah, my old man could've lived in a one room shack, but he bought this place for my mom when she was pregnant with me. They did the whole nuclear family thing until I was ten and my sister was two. Then it all went to hell and my mom skipped town."

It's hard to remember that these badass bikers didn't spring out of an oil stain on a garage floor fully formed and ready to drag their knuckles. I picture a ten year old Noah pushing his baby sister on the swing, waiting for their mom to come back, and my heart nearly breaks. I picture a teenage Noah with milk mustache and prospect vest practicing his scary face in the mirror, and my heart breaks again.

But I can't be sorry for his childhood. "I never had anything like this, Noah. My shithole apartment was an improvement on what I grew up with."

"You don't have to go back there if you don't want. You can stay with the club, even if..."

He doesn't finish and I don't ask him to. I know what he was going to say. *Even if I'm gone.* And by *gone* he means *dead*. But I don't want the club without Noah. He has to know that too. The sun hangs high in the sky, but the porch light still flickers on. Noah lets go of my hand and pulls some keys from his pocket. We stand there on the front step of his father's house for several long seconds in a parody of the end of a first date. Only this isn't an ending. I'm not sure of much, but I'm sure of that.

He pushes my hair out of my eyes, trailing fingertips over my brow and along my jaw. "I just need to see her room and then I'll take you to the safe house."

"I don't want to go to the safe house. If you're not going to be there—" I shake my head "—I don't belong."

"You belong where I put you."

"Even you can't shove a square peg into a round hole."

"The fuck I can't. But you are not a square peg, Star. You liked Drew, didn't you? She'll be there."

"It doesn't matter if I liked her or not. The club could decide to kill you tomorrow. How can I possibly feel safe with them? How can you?"

"You met the club at its most broken and I'm sorry for that, but I have to trust it will be right again. I believe in that brotherhood, baby. I have to. It's all I have."

He pushes the door open and pulls me inside. The living room smells like cinnamon potpourri and pot. Not quite so storybook as I'd imagined. I wonder if the rainbow colored afghan spread over the back of the sofa is a remnant of Noah's mother, or his sister's influence. I can't see his dad putting it there.

A series of school pictures graces the hallway. Noah's start with baby portraits and end around tenth grade. Jules' start at kindergarten and end with a cap and gown. Their transition had to have been rough, but at least Jules had made it to the finish line. I wonder if Noah had just been too cool for yearbook photos. I touch the tassel draped over the graduation photo's frame. I'm pretty sure of the answer, but I ask anyway. "Where's yours?"

"Yeah, school wasn't really for me. How about you?"

"I finished. Even thought I might take some classes at the community college, but that didn't pan out. Not with my hours at the diner."

"Jules started classes this fall, but I think she majored in getting wasted with a minor in advanced napping."

A pulse of anger slices through my sadness. I don't even know her but it hurts me that she'd waste an opportunity I'd have killed to have. I choke back the inappropriate jealousy. Her life isn't all sunshine and roses...even if her front yard is exactly that.

"Do you still have a bedroom here?"

"We don't have time to christen that bed."

"That's not what I had in mind. Can't a girl get a peek at your power ranger sheets? Or are you afraid it'll ruin your image?"

"Baby, this isn't an image. This is who I am. Besides, my sheets were Wrestlemania."

"Of course they were."

He pushes open the door at the end of the hall and a cloud of cucumber melon body spray rolls out. "God, did she bathe in that shit?"

I sniff. The chemical fragrance makes my nose itch, but I recognize something darker underneath. "She was hiding her own pot habit. Your dad probably wouldn't have noticed, considering his."

Her bed is rumpled and her dresser is covered with cosmetics bottles and folded papers. It's kind of a mess, but the type of mess usually left behind by a teenage girl. The only clue that she'd been taken was the playing card whoever took her left behind.

"It doesn't make sense, Star. If the Jokers took her for leverage, they'd have asked for something in return by now."

"Could it be a game? Could someone have screwed up?"

"I don't know enough about their operation to be sure. They're a young club. Only active for fifteen years. No history means no one really can predict what will happen next. Knowing they've been pushing into our territory...it's not good. I don't have a clue who all the players are."

And then it hits me. All those nights closing with Harry. Those long rides home. I might know some of the players. At least I could point them out. "I think I can help with that, Noah."

I tell him my plan and his face hardens into a stone mask. Even his soft lips are forbidding. "No."

"Take me back to the diner, Noah. I can point out the people Harry used to meet out back. I don't have to talk to them. Or we can ride the back roads and I can show you where he stopped to drop things off or pick things up. It's probably the picking up spots you're most interested in, but I'm not sure how I'd have known the difference."

"What am I supposed to do with you if we find trouble?"

"This is recon, Noah. I thought that's what you did, gathered all the information first, right down to the color of the panties we were supposed to wear under our uniforms."

"Don't tell me how to do my job." There's a warning in his voice I haven't heard before. I've skirted too close to a boundary I shouldn't cross. I pull back.

"Fine. Maybe there's more information here. Check under her bed. I'll look at the mess on her dresser." I feel horrible trying to put off my trip to the safe house, because it means putting off Noah's efforts to find his sister, but I can't help it.

I don't really think I'll find anything important amidst the love notes and gum wrappers. I brush my hands over the sleek mahogany wood and flick the glass drawer pulls. The furniture is beautiful. Like something out of a doll's house come to life. The narrow top drawer glides open, revealing a froth of lacy underwear and a beautiful leather diary. Unlocked.

I shouldn't peek. I should not. But jealousy and curiosity overwhelm me. I flip through the pages edged in gold leaf. I can't help it.

I shouldn't.

My own words echoed back in looping cursive jolt me.

He came to my window again. I shouldn't have let him in, but I did.

"Noah." My pulse pounds and my finger flies over the page, tracing her secret confessions. "Noah, I don't think she was taken. Well, not for leverage."

I hand him the diary and watch his stony face crack as he catches up on all the players. Jules has found herself one dangerous Romeo.

FIVE

Zig tosses the diary across the bar to Noah's dad. "It's a punk move, but it's still a move on the club. If he only wanted to get his dick wet, he wouldn't have left a calling card in her bed."

"I'd appreciate it if you'd refrain from talking about wet dicks and my daughter's bed in the same sentence."

Zig exhales a cloud of sweet smoke and holds the joint out. "That ship has sailed, old man."

Pop's lip curls but he doesn't follow through with any harsh words. Instead, his shoulders droop and he sighs heavily as he accepts the smoke. "So what's our play now that we know who has her? Diplomacy? Go in guns blazing?"

Zig looks to Noah. "What do you think?"

"There's nothing more dangerous than teenagers in love." Noah drains his beer in two long pulls and slams the bottle. "We can't underestimate them and we can't let the Jokers think we'll let any of this stand. They need to pay."

I've been practicing my inconspicuous look at the end of the bar. So far they've forgotten I'm here, and I don't want to remind them. I'll get sent to bed. Or worse, get shipped off to the safe house on the back of someone's bike. But I have to say something. *Pay doesn't mean writing a check.* "I know this kid. He used to wash dishes at Jimmy's. He was a hothead, but he was never violent."

Noah cups the back of my neck, teasing at the fine hair along my nape. I lean into the warmth of his touch. "He probably wasn't hooked up with the Jokers when you knew him. An MC can take a man with a short fuse and turn him into a precision weapon."

All the men look away at that admission. Zig scrubs a hand over his face and rakes at his beard. "He's probably making his bones with this shit. Stealing the daughter of a former club president, the sister of a current club enforcer, takes some enormous balls. Hugely stupid giant balls. Even if she's willing to go. Ten bucks says this kid is holed up somewhere with Jules, pissing his pants now that he's had a chance to think about what he's done."

I can imagine that easily—young lovers taking things too far, losing their heads, making a mess they don't know how to fix. "There's an abandoned trailer out on county road twenty that the kitchen staff sometimes used for partying. I don't know if it's still there, but it'd be my first stop.

Zig looks at me for the first time since we settled at the bar. "Can you show me on the map, honey?"

"Yeah. But it'd be easier to take you."

Noah's hand stills and my muscles tense. I'm no longer being petted for meaningful contributions to the conversation. "What part of 'you are not fucking coming' is so hard to understand, Star?"

I sit very still, jaw tight. "I'm sorry wanting to help pisses you off so much."

"Baby, either you're stupid and you think this is all some kind of game or you *want* to get yourself killed. I'm pretty sure you're not stupid."

"Fuck you."

Noah's father whistles through his teeth. "You better get your girl in line, son."

Your girl. Noah doesn't correct him, or argue with him. I'm his girl.

I shouldn't like that right now, but I do. It fills my chest up with something warm and sweet. I hold it there with one deep breath and it lifts me higher than a hit off the joint Noah's dad and Zig have been passing back and forth. Then Noah's hand twists into my hair. He's not quite pulling, just gathering it up enough to tug at my scalp. A reminder of what he can do to me and how I respond. My whole body goes hot—with shame, with embarrassment, and with arousal.

"Fucking me is on the list of acceptable activities." From the corner of my eye I see Zig studying us both. His bloodshot eyes are narrowed, but there's a wicked glint in them. Beneath his beard, I'm pretty sure he's smiling. My cheeks heat even more wondering if it's my mouth amusing him or Noah's rough correction. "Along with bringing me food, folding my underwear, and doing what I god damn tell you."

That stings. Then I remember him bringing me breakfast this morning, carrying the steaming plate from the kitchen and feeding me eggs. What had changed? Only Stone was sitting at the bar with us then. Somehow realizing that this is about saving face pisses me off even more.

"Showing off for your friends?" I hiss. "Don't worry, your knuckles still drag when you walk."

As soon as the words are out of my mouth, I regret them. God, maybe I have gone stupid. Maybe it's a contact buzz. His position with the club is in jeopardy and Zig is one of the ones who will be deciding his fate. Have I made him look weak?

Before I can decide if I need to apologize, he pulls me toward him, forcing me to slide off my bar stool and stand awkwardly beside him. Pissing me off all over again.

His mask—cold menace and control—slams firmly back in place. "We're going to finish this conversation in private."

SIX

Noah hustles me down the hallway, his hand never leaving my hair. I can feel my own fuse shortening, anger bubbling up to drown out some of the lust. The club is almost empty. Most of the men are moving their loved ones to safety in case of a turf war. They're unaware that what we'd thought was a kidnapping is a little more ambiguous.

Because his sister is wild and irresponsible. Because *she* wanted to play on the dark side. And yet I'm the one he's mad at? No.

He kicks the door shut behind us and releases me. I stumble and land on my knees beside the bed.

"Say what you want in private, but you should know there's a price to pay for mouthing off to me in public like that." His belt is off with a *whoosh* and then his pants are open.

"Gonna shut me up with your cock?"

"If that's what it takes."

It's easy to fall into this rhythm with him. To let anger turn to lust. To fuck instead of talking. His cock, hard and insistent, throbs between us. I circle it with my fingers and lick the tip. Doing a good job is the last thing on my mind, though. I suck him into my mouth and release him with a pop just as quickly.

"Quit screwing around."

"You're a bastard."

He nods, tucking himself back into his pants. "Not gonna argue that."

Of course not. How could he? It's the truth. He grabs me by my shoulders and pulls me up onto the bed. "And I'm not going to apologize for wanting to protect you. You need to learn a few things."

"Oh yeah? Well you need to learn some things too. You need to learn that I'm a person. A smart person. With ideas and—and—" His stubble grazes the delicate skin of my neck and I draw in a shuddering breath. "That's not fighting fair."

"Bastards don't follow rules."

"Liar."

"I follow the rules that suit me. The club suits me. I understand it better than any follow-the-speed-limit closed-after-sunset bullshit. Brotherhood. Loyalty to people who've earned it by blood or by deed." He nips my shoulder—marking me—and forces me to look at him. He's all dark smile and hooded eyes. "Everyone else can go to hell."

"Because you'll send them there?" My voice quivers because I'm thinking about Harry. I can't help it. And the kid I used to work with who's obviously stupid and dangerous but possibly in love with Jules.

Noah moves so fast I barely have time to gasp before I'm on my back. He's hovering over me, hands planted on either side of my body, face inches from mine.

"They find their own way. Drugs, gambling—you think we picked Harry up on his way to teach Sunday school? Shit. None of them are innocent." His breath fans hot against my cheek and then he brings his mouth to my ear, stubble and velvet skin tickling me as he whispers. "And if a little lost kitten lands in my path, do you know what I do?"

I lick my lips and squirm beneath him. He's talking about me now and I think I know the answer he wants. The one that paints him a monster.

You eat it. It's right there on the tip of my tongue. But it's a lie.

"You snarl. And you growl." I buck my hips up, grinding against the knee he's got planted between my legs. "And you tell them to run."

"But you didn't." He collapses on top of me, crushing me with his body. Every inch of him is a burden I will gladly bear.

"Kittens rarely do what you tell them to do." I push until he lifts up enough that I can see his face. "I'm not a kitten, Noah. I'm not innocent. I've done things…" I squeeze my eyes shut, unwilling to face my own darkness. "My mother's boyfriends. Sometimes I let them—it was easier than explaining a bloody lip or—or—worse. When I left, I stole her rent money from a coffee can under the sink. Just like the one I have now. And Officer Wade—"

"Baby. Stop."

My stomach, already churning with fear and disgust at my confessions, drops. Even he doesn't want to hear what I've done. I turn my face into the pillow. "Loyalty, family. Those are what you believe in and I didn't have a drop of loyalty for mine."

"Family may get loyalty by default, but they sure as hell can lose it. You should've been protected." He grips my chin and pulls me back to face him. His lips are so soft against mine. It's barely a kiss.

"I'm not innocent. I'm not loyal. And I don't know when to keep my mouth shut. How can you possibly still want me?"

"You're a survivor, Star. You're brave and strong. Wild and sweet. You're sexy as hell and you're mine. How could I *not* want you?"

This rhythm is even easier. The one where he caresses my face. The one where he rolls us over until I'm sprawled on top of him. The one where he pins me tight to his chest and our hearts thump against each other.

I slip my hand under his shirt and slide my fingers over the ridges of his abdomen, up the hard planes of his pecs. I want to touch that crazy thunder and feel the heat of him without any barrier between us. He covers my hand with his own, holding me there.

I know we can't stay like this much longer.

Outside of Noah's room, chaos waits to claim us. But for a moment we have stillness. We have peace. Together.

There's a buzzing against my hip, and just like that the moment is over. Noah jostles me to the side so he can pull the phone from his pocket. "Your ride to the safe house is here."

"I don't want to leave you—" He tenses beneath me. "Not because I think I can help. I know I can't do anything. It's just...I'm afraid I won't see you again."

"Maybe you won't, but I promise I'll be trying my damnedest to get back to you."

SEVEN

A big black truck with a wrecked bike on the flatbed idles in front of the club. The hood is covered in stylized flames surrounding a silver logo. DH Towing.

The wind shifts and—along with the twangy country music rolling out of the open windows— I'm struck with the scent of exhaust and stale body odor. Before I take two more steps toward it, my skin crawls. I know who's behind the wheel. Dale, with his filthy beard and portable spittoon.

I can't get in the cab with him. I cannot.

Noah squeezes my hand. "Don't worry, I wouldn't send you alone with Dale. Stone's going with you too. They'll drop you off and head back to catch up with us. Pick up any wrecks we leave in our wake."

"Is that Stone's bike?" I try not to think about Noah, battered and broken, clinging to a hunk of twisted metal on the side of the road. "This doesn't feel right."

"It isn't supposed to."

Noah kisses my forehead. Warmth suffuses me, chasing away some of the dread roiling in my belly.

The passenger door pops open and Stone waves me up. "See what a good guy I am? I'm sitting bitch so you don't have to snuggle this dirty bastard."

"Thank you, I guess."

One last kiss, one last touch, and Noah boosts me up. I grab the handle by the seat and hoist myself the rest of the way. Noah swats my ass and slaps the side of the truck. "Remember. Keep 'em to yourself, motherfucker, or I'll take my boot to your clutch hand."

Stone laughs. "I know the drill."

Dale grunts and I refuse to look at him. Noah and Stone may not have a problem with him, but after what he said in the meeting this morning I certainly do. Never mind the fact that he creeps me out.

The cab of the truck is too warm, even with both windows rolled down. Two big men crowding the enclosed space, both smokers and drinkers, one of them looking very much like a shower isn't part of his daily routine.

I lean as close to the open passenger side window as I can without hanging my head outside like a pet. It's hard to resist.

Stone stays true to his word and keeps his hands planted firmly on his own thighs.

"Where are we going?"

Dale snorts. "Wouldn't be very safe if we told anyone who asked, would it?"

"It's not like you've got a bag over my head. I'm going to see when we get there."

Stone elbows me in the ribs. "Don't give him ideas."

We ride along the familiar stretch of highway in silence. When Dale takes the exit that leads to Jimmy's Diner, I shift in my seat. Stone's body goes rigid beside me. "What's going on, brother?"

"Gotta take a leak."

"You can't wait another fifteen minutes?"

"Wouldn't be stopping if I could, now would I?"

I scrunch down in my seat. It's surreal to be heading back to Jimmy's now. Has the anger over me not showing up for work turned into fear for my wellbeing yet? It usually takes a few days around here. One or two days could too easily be a bender. I suppose I could call this a bender, except instead of booze I've been drunk on lust. Only all that lust has turned into something more. Not quite love, but it feels like it could be someday.

Dale parks us on the side of the restaurant and leaves the truck running when he hops out. "Stay put. I'll drain the snake and grab some pie."

Neither of us respond to him. I guess he's beneath contempt for both of us.

Sitting outside Jimmy's reminds me of how abruptly I'd left.

I didn't say goodbye to a soul. I didn't have anyone I was really close to, but I'd gone out with the girls more than a few times. We chatted about our lives and our troubles in between customers. Sometimes we gossiped about each other. We bickered and fought like siblings. They were kind of a family for me too.

I could say goodbye now. Or at least see if anyone has missed me. But I doubt a trip down memory lane is a good excuse for leaving the car when I'm technically on lock down.

I turn to Stone, whose eyes are fixed on the road that runs parallel to the diner. "Would it be all right if I ran in to see if they're holding my paycheck? Real fast. While Dale's still inside."

It isn't an outright lie. They very well might be holding my paycheck. Not that I'd make a special trip for my below-minimum-wage earnings. My checks usually run between twenty and eighty dollars for well over full time, thanks to tips and the inhumane wage the state lets businesses pay servers. I hold my breath.

Stone doesn't take his eyes off the road. "Yeah. But be quick about it."

I'm out of the cab like a shot before he can change his mind and before Dale can come back out.

I'll just say hi to the girls and let them know I'm still alive in case they were wondering. No big deal.

The bells tinkle over the front door, announcing my entrance.

The restaurant is eerily quiet. Only one customer in the whole place. A sad old man with his sad old pot roast special. Dale is nowhere to be seen.

Ella, one of the newer servers, leans against the coffee bar marrying the ketchup bottles. "Star! Where the hell have you been?"

Relief washes over me—that someone noticed I'd been gone, that someone cared. I don't know Ella very well at all but I want to wrap my arms around her, squeeze her, and tell her everything. I open my mouth to do just that but headlights flash in the window reminding me this is not a social call.

"Long story." I scan for Dale, unsure if it would be better to see him or not. I shake my head. Knowing is better. Knowing is *always* better. "Did you talk to a dirty old biker who came in here just a few minutes ago?"

"Yeah. Weird as shit. He asked where the bathrooms were, then he dodged through the kitchen instead and went right out the back door. Didn't make any sense."

Fuck. Everything about this smells rotten. I race through the front doors, needing to warn Stone so he can get back to Noah as much as I need to breathe.

As I round the corner outside, I hear sirens approaching the side of the restaurant I'd just come from. *Shit.* I press myself flat against the side of the building and peek around the corner.

Maybe they're just hungry. Or they're cutting through the parking lot to get somewhere else. Both scenarios seem ridiculous, but they're all I've got to hold on to for several long minutes until the cruiser stops.

I peek again. Officer Wade is pulling Stone out of the truck. I can't hear what they're saying. Not over the loud radio and the sirens. But I can guess.

"I'm sorry, Stone," I whisper to myself and barrel back into the restaurant.

I dive straight for the cabinet beside the register where we sometimes keep our purses. "You got a car here, Ella? I'm going to need your keys."

"Excuse me?"

"Your keys. It's an emergency." I find a purple leather satchel that has to belong to Ella, and start digging. I don't care what she says, I'm taking her car. I need to find Noah. I need to warn him.

Ella's keys rattle at the bottom of the bag and I fish them out. I'm afraid to run through the kitchen in case any of the cooks or busboys are connected to Dale. I can't go around the outside of the building without making myself a target for Wade.

Wade is the greater of the evils, I decide. And push through the double swinging doors. Ella screams after me, "Don't you dare hurt my baby! I saved for two years to buy that piece of shit."

"I'll be careful," I assure her. But I won't be. My right foot is already itching for the gas pedal.

Noah is going to be furious with me if I find him. *Dale is a traitor. Wade has Stone.* I repeat it over and over in my head so I can say it in one breath. Ella's little Civic is a dull grey and the lining on the roof droops low in spots. There are tacks in some places holding it up. I don't expect much, but the engine purrs to life.

I slam it into reverse and peel out of the parking lot in a cloud of dust and gravel.

Dale is a traitor. Wade has Stone.

I know where Noah was headed with the rest of the club, to the abandoned trailer I pointed out on the map. God, it could be a trap. *Dale is a traitor. Wade has Stone.*

They're probably already there. I shake my head against the unwelcome thought and squeeze the steering wheel even more tightly. I have to assume they're moving slow or got sidetracked. I have to assume there's still hope.

I press down on the accelerator until it touches the floorboard. I've never driven this fast, but I don't have a choice. *Dale is a traitor. Wade has Stone.*

Noah needs me.

HOLD ME DOWN

PART 4 OF 4

ONE

There's a split-second when a fist is flying at your face—right before impact—that you have a choice. Tense up and suffer more or let it happen. Take it. Roll with the punch.

I'm done rolling. I'm done going limp and taking whatever blows life hands me.

It might hurt more, but I'm going to fight.

That's what I tell myself as my headlights slice a path in the darkness. With no weapon but my wits, and no plan but *faster-forward-now*, I turn down the back road that will take me to an abandoned trailer. The one I identified on a map for Noah earlier today.

Gravel crunches under the tires as the road shifts to driveway. I half expect to see emergency lights and hear sirens in the distance, but everything that made this place a perfect spot to party means all of that is unlikely. The nearest neighbors are a five minute drive away at least.

I've got a ways to go before I see the trailer, but finally my headlights catch on something other than a flash of tree or swath of road. The reflectors on six or seven parked bikes glint in the darkness.

A mixture of shock and relief washes over me. I did it. I got here in time to let Noah know this could all be a trap. In time to save him. Maybe. I hope.

I don't know for sure who those bikes belong to, but I take a calculated risk and roll to a stop beside them.

Two men peel out of the darkness. Noah's silhouette is unmistakable. I've run my hands over every inch of his body. I'd know him anywhere. The burly man beside him must be Zig. They're at my door—guns drawn—in seconds.

Noah's voice rumbles over me. "Lights off. Get the fuck out of the car. Nice and slow—"

I scramble for the switch to kill the lights and pop my seatbelt. Halfway out of the car, I can hear the faint thump of music drifting down from a party.

Then Noah is on me, pulling me from the front seat and pinning me to the rear driver's side door. ".Jesus, Star. What the hell are you doing here?"

"The cops grabbed Stone."

"And they just let you wander off?"

The metal is cold against my back, making Noah's heat against the front of me a raging furnace. I push into that furnace, shove into the heat and muscle with my body and breath. "No, I got out of the truck before it happened, and don't give me any shit for that. If I hadn't, I'd be spending time with Officer Wade right now."

"Did he put his hands on you?" Noah's eyes flash bright with rage. With fear? No that can't be it. Noah isn't afraid of Wade. Not like me. He'd tossed Wade around the diner parking lot like a bag of trash.

"I told you I got away. It doesn't matter—"

"The hell it doesn't." There's murder in his voice. The uneven timbre of a man on the edge. "Details, Star. Now."

Shoving at him does nothing but make him curve his lips into a dangerous smile. I do it anyway, fighting for an inch more space between us. Room to breathe. "Then let me fucking talk, caveman. Dale took off through the kitchen at Jimmy's. He—" I grab Noah's face and tug him down to me, so I can graze my lips over his ear and whisper.

"He set us up. When I saw Stone getting dragged into a cruiser, I—I borrowed a car. You can't go into that party. They might know you're coming."

Even in the darkness, this close I can see Noah's body tense. Watch his eyes narrow. Feel the muscles under my hands shift. He pulls me into a hug, and I'm not sure if he's comforting me or taking comfort for himself. As I sink into his granite arms and press my face to the leather over his chest, I'm not sure it matters. The adrenaline coursing through my blood and propelling me straight into danger recedes, leaving me light-headed. He turns to Zig and they have a whole conversation in grunts.

"Dale." Noah spits the traitor's name like a curse.

Zig leans against the car, settling his bulky body beside us. "That piece of shit."

"Yeah."

Zig crushes a cigarette under his boot heel, carefully picks up the butt, and tucks it into his pocket. For a second I'm confused. Is Zig worried about litter? And then it dawns on me that he's worried about evidence. He dusts his hands on his jeans and points to me. "You sure she's..."

My heart hammers against my ribs at Zig's unfinished question. He could be wondering about my intelligence or my ability, but we all know it's really my loyalty that's on shaky ground. I don't blame him. Everyone's loyalty is uncertain now.

Noah squeezes me tight against his chest. Like I'm a toy and Zig might try to take me away. "Do. Not. Go there."

"All right, brother. She's right anyway. He probably already called ahead. Warned these tweakers."

"I'm not leaving without my sister."

"We don't even know if—"

"If she's not, someone in there knows where she is. I will bust heads like piñatas until answers fall out."

Zig's mouth settles into a hard line. "Fine. What about her?"

"We're gonna need the cargo space if Jules is…" he brushes his knuckles against my cheek and squeezes his eyes shut. "Hurt."

My stomach turns at the thought. My heart is still holding out hope that these are star-crossed lovers. That Jules wasn't taken by force. Zig heads back to the rest of their crew.

They know what they're doing. They have all the information. I did my part. Mission accomplished. Why don't I feel relieved? Because they're still walking into the unknown. And because Noah's fate is still undecided. These men are with him now, but they still get to vote on whether he lives or dies for killing their insane president.

Noah untangles himself from my body. "It'd be a wasted fucking effort, sending you away, wouldn't it?"

I nod.

"You're going to take this crappy grocery basket with an engine, point it south, and wait at the end of the driveway. You keep it running. You keep it in drive. And you keep your foot on the brake until me or Jules tells you to go." He cups my face and locks his eyes on mine, like he's trying to see the back of my soul. "Remember what she looks like?"

The graduation portrait is still fresh in my mind so I nod again.

"Good girl." Noah kisses me. The warmth of his praise and the brush of his lips wash over me, soothing away the last jagged edge of my terrible adrenaline rush. And then he's pressing cool metal into my hand. "Do you know how to use this?"

A gun.

"I—" Do I know how to use it? I know the way cats know how to flex their claws. But I also know the last time I had a gun in my hand I couldn't pull the trigger. And I should have. I should have blasted that fucker all over my bedroom wall.

As my fingers curl around the textured grip, it's *his* voice that rings in my ears.

"Oh, aren't you a big girl? Does that gun feel as good in your hands as my prick?"

No. It does not feel good. Not the gun. Not the prick. I shake my head and draw back the safety.

They're all the same. Pointing one gun or another at me. Teaching me to use them like it's a favor. Like I wanted the lesson. "It's over. No more."

"Over? It's never over. Not for gutter trash girls like you, Star. Shoot me. Squeeze that big gun in your dirty little hands and put a bullet in me while I'm holding your sweet sixteen present."

I don't tell him that it's not my birthday—that I turned seventeen last month—because he doesn't care. I don't tell him that he's wrong, either. Because he isn't. I am trash and my hands are so filthy I can hardly look at them. I've done terrible things. If I kill him? There's not enough soap in the world to scrub them clean.

"Do it," he urges. "You'll go to jail."

"It's self-defense." I cry, but I'm already letting the nose of the gun dip toward the floor.

He drops the present and grabs the gun. Then backs slowly out of the room. "You know what we do to dogs that bite the hands that feed them? We lock them up until they learn their lesson. And if they can't learn, Star? We put them to sleep."

I didn't shoot him because I was too weak and too scared. That's not a problem I need to worry about any more. I shake off the memory and set my jaw. I'm strong now. I tell myself over and over and over. Eventually, I'll believe it.

"Yeah, I know how to use it." The gun is a solid weight in my palm. Not too heavy. Already warming to my skin. My hand barely shakes. "Feels good."

TWO

The digital clock in the cracked dashboard slips from 11:10 to 11:11, and the childish urge to make a wish grabs me low in my belly. Maybe it's the gun, the constant danger, the uncertainty, all of it swirling together in this terrible miasma of nostalgia and grief, but I would wish on anything right now.

Eyelashes.   Flickering   lights.   Broken bones. *Anything.* If it brought Noah back safe.

Darkness surrounds me, but my eyes have adjusted enough that I can make out leaves rustling in the brush line. Shadows tearing around the bend in the drive. My whole body tenses. I fight the urge to lift my foot off the brake and roll away. That shadow could be Noah with Jules or one of our people.

Our people? When had they become mine too? Had they?

I think about traitorous Dale, so much like the men I'd found half dressed in my kitchen so many mornings growing up. Eating my Fruit Loops and looking at me like I was the unwelcome prize at the bottom of the cereal box. Or worse, a welcome prize.

I think about Dev and the sick crack of his neck. No, they aren't my people. But those two men aren't here, either. They aren't the club. Not anymore.

I flex the fingers of my left hand on the steering wheel and stroke the pistol grip with my right.

The shadows draw closer and closer. And then it's a thump against the door. A man's hand against the window. I let out a little shriek.

"It's all right, Star. Noah sent me to make sure Jules found you okay. You know getaway drivers usually leave the doors unlocked, right?" I recognize the prospect from back at the club. And Jules beside him, moonlight glinting off of her dark hair, looking younger than her senior portrait but also more jaded.

"Shit. Sorry." I apologize while rolling down the window a little and popping the locks. She tumbles into the backseat.

"Take me back to my house."

I turn to the prospect still standing outside the car. "That can't be safe, can it?"

"It's fine. No other stops though." He slaps the roof and heads back up the driveway.

"Don't worry. They're not at war." Jules shoves a plastic bag full of laundry to the floor and yanks at the seatbelt. "The Jokers are a bullshit club. Candy asses. Didn't take more than some busted down doors and a few warning shots. They dropped to their knees for The Devil's Host faster than back alley hookers."

"Are you okay? Did they—were you hurt?"

Our eyes lock in the rear view mirror and she jerks her head. A stiff movement that emphasizes the sharpness of her jaw line and reminds me of her brother. "No permanent damage. Except maybe to my pride. I won't make the mistake of falling for a bunch of lines from a pretty boy biker ever again, that's for sure."

"You know it's not your fault, right? No matter what anyone says."

"I knew better."

"No. He knew better. You just opened your damn heart. You wanted something more. There's nothing wrong with that."

"Okay, Dr. Phil. Now get us out of here. It may not be war but The Jokers are going to have to make restitution. They'll be talking business for hours."

I'm relieved, but there's an undercurrent of disappointment. That I didn't get to contribute. That my drive had been for nothing. I look at the exhausted young woman in the back seat and my heart aches for her.

The drive is slow and silent until a flash of red and blue glints in the rearview mirror. My stomach twists into a familiar knot of dread. Jules kicks the back of my seat. "Hide that gun before you pull over."

Shit. I shove the gun under a canvas grocery bag tucked between the seats and glide to the shoulder. Sweat prickles under my arms and on my palms. A sour taste floods my mouth. I roll down the window and keep my chin tucked to my chest, speaking softly, making myself as small as possible. "What seems to be the—"

"License and registration, ma'am."

A burst of icy dread jolts down my spine at the familiar voice. Officer Wade.

He points a flashlight in the window and I am blinded for a moment. I still manage to keep my face averted. Maybe he won't recognize me. My clothes are different. My hair. Half the time people don't recognize me at all outside of the restaurant, even when I tell them who I am. That desperate hope flutters in my chest as I flip open the glove compartment. I say a tiny prayer of thanks that Ella has a neat little folder marked "car documents." Registration, insurance card, and— jackpot—her license too. Instead of fishing mine out, I hand him the entire contents of the folder. Ella and I have the same hair and eye color. She's a little shorter than me, but sitting down I don't think he'll be able to tell.

I hold my breath while he inspects everything. He flicks the ultra-bright light back into the car and glides it over Jules. "How about you, Miss? ID."

"Oh, I lost my pursh," she slurs like a buzzed sorority sister and slips a little lower in the seat. "At the party. I love my safe ride. Take me home, safe ride."

"Party? Have you ladies been drinking?"

"No. I—I—I—"

"I said she was my safe ride." Jules' voice sharpens.

"Step out of the car, Miss."

I consider making a run for it, but Wade's got his gun drawn before I can even get my hand halfway to the ignition. "Step out of the car. Now."

As soon as I'm out of the car his hand is wrapped around my upper arm and he's dragging me toward the back of the vehicle. "Did you think I wouldn't know who you were? Really? How stupid do you think I am, Star?"

I grunt in response. There's no way I'm walking into that one.

"And how fucking stupid are you? You're in so much trouble."

"You didn't even have a reason to pull me over," I shout, all my nerve bubbling over.

"Really?" His hand flies out and plastic crunches under the butt of his flashlight. Red-orange shards skitter across the ground. "You had a busted tail light. Then you used a false identity. Probable DUI. Don't worry, I've got a flask that says by the time anyone finds you, you'll be blowing well above the legal limit. We'll have a little party of our own."

There's an ugly purple bruise on his forehead, and I can't help but laugh. I can't believe I'd felt guilty for what Noah had done to him. He'd deserved it. And more. "Noah's going to kill you."

"Did someone knock your little noggin against the headboard one too many times? Noah. Is. Not.

Here. I've got it on good authority he's indisposed at the moment."

Oh, God. Are the cops back at the trailer? Or is Wade dirtier than I thought? "What do you know?"

He jerks me toward his police cruiser. "Enough. Hands on the hood. Spread 'em. If you have anything sharp in your pockets, tell me now. I don't like surprises."

"No," I hiss. The hood is warm against my palms, and I focus on that rather than the slide of Wade's hands over my hips and outer thighs.

For a few moments I think he's going to at least do this by the book, then he pats my inner thighs more slowly. He cups my sex and presses his chest into my back.

His breath skims hot and dark over my neck and ear. A sick slide I'd do anything to get away from. "I wanted to save you, Star. I wanted to drag you out of that filthy bastard's clutches and be your hero. But you could ruin a wet dream, couldn't you? This will work too, though. I can make all your problems go away. Just be sweet."

Sweet. God, how many times had I been told to be sweet over the years. To be nice. To be kind. And quiet.

"You created my problems." My tears drop fat and hot against the warm metal and I will my body to go numb to his touch.

"No, no, no," he shushes and pulls me close, licking a trail from my cheek up to the corner of my eye. "You did this to yourself. You should've let me save you, Star. You should've let me love you."

My head spins and I start to slip into that quiet place. The one where nothing can touch me. The one where I can survive anything. But now I know that place isn't real.

All of it had hurt, I'd just delayed feeling it.

I'd done what I had to do in the past, but I'm not the same person anymore. I'm not a scared little girl. I'm not alone.

This hurts. *Now.* I don't have to go numb to survive it. What I have to do is fight.

I throw my elbow back into his ribs, and the startled *oof* he makes is rewarding. The way he stumbles back, surprised and flailing, even more so. I'd caught him off guard enough to roll off the hood and scramble behind my car before he gets his gun drawn again. Jules holds her phone up to the window and I can see the last round of messages between her and someone from the club. From Noah.

Hold tight. I'm coming.

Relief slams into me. That Noah is okay and that he's on his way to help us. I'm dizzy with it. I crouch low to the ground, hugging the side of the car and sliding toward the front passenger door. Drawing Wade toward Jules is the last thing I want to do, but I need to get the gun. I need it like I need air to breathe. Maybe more. Noah gave it to me to protect myself and I do not intend to disappoint him.

Wade takes his time rounding the car. He thinks he's a cat toying with a half dead mouse. He's underestimating me, thank God. I open the passenger side door and reach—

Bang! Bang!

My heart nearly explodes in my chest and everything goes ringing quiet. The car lurches as the rear tires deflate.

"I'm only getting started, you bitch. You're not going anywhere."

My lips curl back into a rictus of a smile as I dig the gun from between the seats.

Jules hisses at me from the backseat clutching her phone. "What are you doing? Noah's on his way."

It will be okay. I mouth the words to her and slip back out of the car. "I'm done with people like you, Wade. People who prey on the weak like it's fun. You're not a predator. You're fucking sick. You're a rabid dog."

He rounds the rear of the vehicle. I see his gun pointed at the ground first, then the length of his arm, the tops of his shoes. "You were always so polite at the diner," Wade hisses. "I guess it was for show. I'm gonna enjoy teaching you some manners."

His eyes widen in shock when he sees me holding the gun.

And if they can't learn, we put them to sleep. The thought blinks through my mind as I squeeze the trigger. Once. Twice. Three times.

Wade drops to the ground. And I take a few steps toward him.

In a horror movie, I'd scream at the girl to run away. *Don't get close to the monster. It's a trap.* But now I understand why they do it. They have to see what they've done. They need to know for sure.

Wade's face is slack. His uniform is rumpled and there are dark splotches spreading where I shot him. His chest doesn't rise or fall. His hands don't reach to grope me. I don't need to touch him to know that's he's dead, but I want to. I drop to my knees beside him, still holding the gun in one hand, and press a finger to one of the bullet holes. It sinks in just a little. I'm invading his body the way he invaded mine. It's hot. Gross. But some sick, twisted place deep in my gut is pleased.

I lean in close, wipe my finger on his cheek, and whisper in his dead ear. "You can't hurt me ever again. No one can."

And then, just as fast, the pleased feeling slips away and my world starts to spin.

THREE

I killed a man.

My vision goes hazy at the edges until all I see are pinpricks. I killed a man. I killed him and I put my finger in a bullet hole.

I'm a monster. A dog. Nothing.

I barely feel Jules tugging the gun from my grip. Noah scooping me into his arms and promising to keep me safe.

I laugh. A wild sound that can't possibly be coming from my throat. What is safe?

He hurt me. He used me. He wanted to do worse.

Noah? Wade? Fuck if I know. They're all the same, aren't they? I laugh some more. It wracks my body exactly the same way sobbing does.

FOUR

It's strange sitting in the club bar less than twenty-four hours after the worst moment of my life. Life and death, the band plays on. But I'm not playing anymore. I'm here in body only.

"Here ya go, Jay Bird." Zig's gruff tone is softer with Jules than with any of the men. He pushes a shot glass full of maraschino cherries across the bar, and Jules wrinkles her nose.

"That doesn't look like bourbon, old man."

He folds his arms over his chest and narrows his eyes. "You used to beg for cherries. You're the reason we have them behind the bar."

"When I was seven." Jules' exasperated huff sounds slightly pleased.

I try to picture a tiny Jules wandering around the club, and I can't even imagine it. She's done nothing but sleep since we got her back from The Jokers. At least that's what Noah had said. I'd spent most of that time sleeping too. And sobbing. "They let you in the bar when you were little?"

As soon as I ask the question, I realize how silly it must sound. This isn't a regular bar with a bouncer at the door and a Happy Hour special. This is a private club. For outlaws. They do whatever they want. And of course I can imagine it. It looks just like this, a sassy little girl giving Zig a hard time.

"Only sometimes. They do cookouts and stuff. Family things." She tucks a strand of glossy dark hair behind her ear and chews the corner of her thumb. The brief mention of family shadows her face. For a moment I'm struck with how alike she and Noah are. She juts her chin at Zig. "Did you check the expiration date on that jar? If those are just for me they might be old enough to vote."

"Nah, these are fresh. Drew's little peanut likes them."

"I see how it is." Her lips quirk into a smile and she pops a piece of the unnaturally red fruit between them. "You've got a silly little nickname for her too. Poor thing'll be stuck with Peanut for life."

"Maybe." Zig's face flashes something I'd almost call bashful—a softness around the corners of his eyes, a little uncertainty at the mouth. Just as quick it's gone. But now I know for sure that he and Drew have something special. Something real. He stands up straighter, snags a bottle of Jim Beam from the wall, and clears his throat. "Noah."

I turn to watch Noah close the distance between us. The crowd parts for him, everyone giving him the right of way. Nodding, clapping him on the shoulder, grunting acknowledgements. It's so different from the first night he brought me here, when we slipped in nearly unnoticed.

Noah steps between me and Jules at the bar and rests his hand at the small of my back. His dark hair is still slick from the shower, skin damp beneath a clean white cotton t-shirt and battered leather cut. I lean into him, wrapping my arm around his waist, inhaling the soap and spice. I take comfort in his body.

Noah nods to Zig. "Set her up. She's earned a drink after what she's been through."

"Wow." Jules sneers. "You're in charge now? I thought Zig suddenly developed a respect for the underage drinking law."

Zig raises a brow at her sarcastic remark and pours three shots. Booze for lunch seems like a perfectly reasonable thing right about now.

Noah nudges a shot toward each of us and grabs one for himself. "Watch the mouth, Jules. After your little adventure, you're going to need my permission to breathe."

Jules and Noah both knock their drinks back with practiced ease while I choke down the burning liquid. She slams the glass down on the bar top and shakes her head. "I want to go bail Stone out."

"No." Noah points to his empty glass, and Zig refills it. Mine too.

"You're always telling me to clean up my own messes. It's my fault he got picked up. I should go bail him out."

Noah tosses back the second shot. "Absolutely not. One, it isn't your fault he got picked up. Two, you don't need to have anything to do with the cops right now. Three, it's not your place."

"What cops? I'll post bail through a bondsman. It's not like I've never done it before. Or should I have left your ass in jail the last time?"

Noah sighs and scrubs a palm over his face. "I don't like it."

"Yeah, well, I'm sure Stone doesn't like spending his weekend in lockup. And no one else is up for the job right now. Or does he have an old lady I don't know about?"

"You sure as hell don't need to be worried about that."

"I'm not." Her cheeks flush pink—maybe from the alcohol, maybe something more—and she pops another cherry. "I just know that if he did have a woman, we wouldn't be having this conversation. You're really gonna leave him hanging like that?"

Noah pulls a money roll from his pocket and peels off several worn hundred-dollar bills. Zig does the same.

"That's what I thought." Jules sweeps the bills into a small pile and tucks them into her pocket. "I'll go make the call in the office."

Jules returns fifteen minutes later with none of the blush left in her cheeks. She drops the cash on the bar top, and I don't think anyone but me notices the slight tremor in her grip. "He's already out."

Zig sets up another round of shot glasses on the bar. "Good. He'll be back for the vote tonight."

The vote that will decide Noah's fate. They're all so matter-of-fact about it, I want to scream. Instead I swallow the burning liquor. It scorches a path all the way to my belly.

FIVE

Enough shots, and my body feels pleasantly floaty. Disconnected from where I am and the things I've done. But not completely. Not enough.

Jules is gone. Zig is working the other end of the bar. I reach for Noah, searching his face for something. "I need..."

Absolution? Oblivion? The kind of raw lust that scorches away everything in its path. Yes, that last one.

"Tell me what you need, baby. Tell me how to help you."

I open my mouth, then close it again. I need too much. I'm beyond help. "I just want it all to go away. Make me forget?"

He spins me around, pulls me onto his lap and guides my arms back, back, back, until my shoulders are straining and my hands are clasped behind him. My chest juts out ahead of us as if I'm a mermaid strapped to the prow of a storybook ship.

"Look at those bastards. You know who they are now and what they're capable of doing."

"Yes." I answer even though he hadn't really asked me a question.

"Would you let any of them fuck you?"

I jerk, shocked. "What kind of question is that?"

"A serious one." His voice is a rough whisper. Only for me. "Tell me, Star. Who would you fuck if I wasn't here?"

I twist in his embrace but he doesn't let me go. I want to scream at him that I wouldn't be here if it weren't for him. Instead I grit my teeth. "I don't like this. It feels like a trap or a test and—screw you. None of them. Not one."

"What if I told you to do it?" There's an edge of playfulness in his voice and my breath catches. A shameful heat spreads through my core at the thought of being used in such a way. A heat spiked with fear. Sharp. Dangerous. Destructive.

"Noah. Don't."

"Star." He mocks my warning tone.

"Are you planning to give me away? Is this business? Am I going to be a gift with purchase?" I don't want to be used for business. Pleasure, yes. His pleasure especially. "I won't be a pawn."

"No baby. Like a gift, period."

His grip on my arms softens and my heart thunders. "Why?"

"Because you're mine to give. Makes my dick hard just thinking about you spreading your legs and taking whatever cock I tell you to take. And because I think you like the idea. Your nipples are so fucking tight right now, I can see them through your shirt."

His stubble grazes my neck and I shiver. "Who?" I ask.

"Those guys. Playing pool."

I study them. Big and tattooed. Scary. Neither of them with anything to give. Except their loyalty, and Noah already has that.

"Maybe I'd let them drape you over the green felt and each take turns holding you down while the other fucks your sweet pussy."

I can imagine the abrasion of the rough fabric against my nipples, their thick fingers digging into my thighs, the smell of beer and ashes invading my nostrils as I pant. I can play this game with him.

"Just my pussy?" I breathe.

"Fuck, Star." He groans. Now it's his turn to squirm. "That mouth of yours. All I want to do is fill it with cock. Or kiss it."

209

"Would you do that? Fill my mouth while—" I jut my chin in the direction of the pool table "—one of them fills me…somewhere else?"

And just like that I'm spinning out of his lap and over his shoulder. My head reels. Heat radiates through my ass cheek and down my thigh. Noah doesn't pull his hand back to spank me again. He holds it there—holds me steady—as he marches toward the exit. "You're in for it now."

"I called your bluff."

"Another man so much as breathes wrong in your direction and I'll use his face to polish my fucking boots."

He carries me out of the club and drives me straight back to the little house on the edge of town.

***

The couch in Noah's father's house smells like motor oil and lemon Pledge. It's a personal, homey smell that shouldn't be so foreign. But it is. The smells of last night—gunpowder, the metallic tang of blood—haunt me. I curl onto my side and draw my knees up to my chest. It's the first quiet moment since the nightmare with Wade that I'm not sobbing. The weight of it settles over me and I shudder.

Noah cradles my head in his lap and strokes my hair. His touch is gentler than it's ever been.

The tenderness puts me on edge so I press my cheek into his denim-covered thigh. "You're touching me like I'm made of glass."

His voice is low and soft. "I'm just trying to take care of you."

"Then hold me like you mean it. You're supposed to be granite, Noah. And I've been trying to break myself against you since I met you. Only it hasn't worked. I must be made of harder stuff than anyone thought."

He presses the rough pads of his fingers into the muscles knotted in my neck. "I knew. I always knew. Even when you were shy, limping in your new work shoes, but refusing to sit down."

"God." My voice cracks. "I'm going to go to prison for the rest of my life."

"Baby, no." He pulls me up until his arms are around me and we're face to face. "You did what needed to be done. You protected my sister. You protected the club. That kind of loyalty is rewarded. It's taken care of."

"I'm not loyal, Noah. Never have been. Not to my family. Not to a job."

He presses his forehead to mine. "Did your family or your boss ever do one fucking thing to earn your loyalty?"

I shake my head.

"That's what I thought. You bailed on all of them but you drove into hell for me. Why?"

I squeeze my eyes shut and tears roll down my cheeks. This is too much. "I don't know."

"Bullshit, Star." He shakes me—not hard—but enough that my eyes spring open and I see him for who he is. A man who won't be denied. Hard and fierce. Mine.

"Because you earned it. You earned my loyalty."

"And now you've earned ours."

The pride in his voice stings, because I don't feel like I deserve it. "I did it for me, though. No one else."

"That's enough of a reason. I'd ink my name into your flesh right now if I could. I'd brand you. You're not glass, baby. You're diamond. I don't want there to be any more doubt. No more confusion. All of this is mine." He skims his hands up my arms and over my shoulders until he's caressing my jaw—gripping my chin. "Every beautiful, unruly inch. Mine since the minute I laid my eyes on you. Mine to take. Mine to hold. And that makes me yours, Star. Tell me I'm wrong."

I lick my lips, tasting phantom gunpowder mixed with salt. "You're not wrong."

He grins and his whole face changes. Softens. I want him to look at me like this always. "My little warrior."

"Not a warrior." I choke on a bittersweet laugh. Maybe I'm not exactly a coward anymore, but I'm not—that. Am I? I try to look away but he jerks me back to full eye contact.

"Hell fucking yes you are. It was kill or be killed, baby. And you chose life. You protected something precious. My heart."

"Your sister." Of course. It's starting to sink in that maybe I'm not a monster. I may never feel good about what I've done...but I truly didn't have a choice.

"I'm forever grateful to you for protecting Jules, but I'm talking about you. You're my heart. Even if you were alone you did the right thing. How many times do I have to say it? A hundred? A thousand? I'll do it until my voice gives out. I'll do it forever. I love you."

Something warm and giddy bubbles up in my chest. Forcing out all but the last shred of my fear. Did he say love? "This all sounds a lot like vows to me."

"Make no mistake, what I'm talking about is more permanent than any bullshit vows. In-fucking-delible, blood and ink."

"Like the blood on my hands?"

213

Noah releases my chin and grabs my wrist. "Here?" He holds my palm up for inspection. "You're perfect."

And then his lips are on my hand, hard and hot. Kissing a trail over my palm, the delicate underside of my wrist, my forearm. Licking me clean of my invisible filth.

He takes one shuddering breath and it's like he's breathing for the both of us. Like we're one person. I bow to meet him, mouth falling open. His tongue slicks against mine and I shiver with the pleasure of it—collapse into it.

He pulls me more firmly onto his lap. I wriggle until I'm straddling him, knees sinking into the couch, looking down on him a little. He grins and slips his hands under my shirt to cup my breasts. He pushes the shirt up further and I grab the hem to finish the job. It drifts to the ground as I thread my hands behind his neck, pushing my breasts closer to his face. He weighs them in his palms, yanks my bra down so my breasts spill out over the top of the cups and squeezes them roughly, then soothes them with the drag of his thumbs. My nipples are hard points in seconds and a sharp ache builds between my legs. I sink down to press that ache against the hard ridge bulging behind his zipper. He draws one stiff nipple into his mouth at my urging and suddenly we're making out in the living room like teenagers, frantic and messy. His fingers dig into the tender flesh of my belly as he tries to pop the button at the top of my fly. He curses, a soft brush of whisker and breath against my cheek, and yanks at the waistband. "Open your damn pants so I can get my hands on your pussy."

My pants slip easily over my hips once I'm standing, and I hook my fingers into my under-wear, taking them down too.

I'm naked in front of him except for my mangled bra. Somehow that's cruder than total nudity and my body flushes with heat. As I reach behind me to unclasp it, my fingers shake. Not from fear, from desire. From eager anticipation. I might as well be completely exposed, while he sits before me fully clothed. And he said he loves me.

He hooks his arm around my thigh and pulls me back toward him so I wobble, fall forward, and have to steady myself on his shoulders. He likes doing that, keeping me off balance. He did it in my apartment, in his room. He'll keep doing it. Making me stumble and holding me steady.

Forever. Love.

He spreads his legs, forcing my knees further apart.

"You know there's a word for what you're do-ing, right?"

"Foreplay."

"Manspreading."

He laughs and slides a hand up my inner thigh and teases his way up to my pussy. "I'm the only man spreading this from now on, little warrior. Got it?"

I nod my agreement.

He traces over the seam of my sex, humming his approval when he finds me wet.

"When we have a place..." his finger delves deeper, gathering moisture at my entrance and slipping it up to circle my clit. He never takes his eyes off my face, just traces lazy loops over and around that bundle of nerves. I bite my lip against the pleasure, afraid my moans might keep him from finishing what he'd started to say.

When we have a place, I silently urge him to continue as I buck my hips. Then his finger is inside me, curved and deep, stroking me from the inside, beckoning. His thumb skips over my clit and I dig my fingers into his shoulders. I can't hold back. "God that feels good."

"I know, baby. You feel like heaven. S'why I'll want you naked all the time. As soon as our door shuts behind you—no clothes."

Our door. Noah dreaming about our future while he pumps his fingers inside me. I'm already on fire, but a new warmth—syrupy and sweet— spreads out from my chest up to my cheeks. "That might not be very practical. I might want to cook a BLT or answer the door for a delivery."

His lips slide into a smile as he brushes them over my breast, eyes still on my face, fingers still stroking.

"We'd come up with some exceptions." He grins, a flash of even white teeth, and then he nips the plump curve.

Fuck, I want this life. The one where Noah is smiling into my naked skin in our imagined home and I'm making BLTs for dinner. Sexy and sweet. Loved. Forever. I feel it like a thundering in my chest, a pulse between my legs, a hot ball of need in my belly.

It's terrifying how much I want it. Wanting anything this much means I don't get to have it— don't deserve it.

His phone chirps and it sounds exactly like fate snatching everything I want away.

He slips it from his pocket with his left hand, his right hand still working between my legs. After a glance at the screen, he drops it on the couch beside us and reaches up to stroke my cheek, as if to smooth away my disappointment. "I gotta check, babe. Unless I'm balls deep or dying. It's all good. Stone made it to the club okay."

"This is how it'll always be, isn't it? Late night phone calls. People dying. I don't think I can…"

Noah goes very still. "What are you saying?"

The words tumble out in a rush before I can think better of them. "Leave with me. Before the club votes. I'm terrified they'll kill you."

His eyes darken. "That's not going to happen."

I run my fingers over his hair, along his neck. I don't even see the whorls of ink covering him anymore. It's all just…him. Mine. "No. But if they'll even hold a vote about whether to kill you now? If they've got your life in their hands like that? It's never over. We're never safe."

"You still don't get it. It's not supposed to be one way, Star. They hold my life because I hold theirs. We have faith in each other."

"I'm not strong enough for that kind of faith."

He works a second finger inside me, then a third, filling and stretching. His thumb is firm against my clit. Insistent. An irresistible force. "I've got enough for the both of us."

I want to believe him more than anything. I want to let go and accept. I want to stay. But it's too hard. Staying is how I get hurt. How I end up trapped in a room like a rabid dog, holding a gun I'm too scared to use. If I stay here I'll only lose him. Maybe not tonight, but eventually.

And still he works between my legs. Winding me tighter and tighter.

"I can't." I cry as the orgasm tears through me and I collapse against Noah's chest.

He strokes my hair while I tremble with the aftershocks. "You can do so much more than you think."

"Don't give me a choice, Noah. Hold me down or send me away. If I have to choose, I'll break both of our hearts."

His laugh rumbles over me, dark and wistful. "I don't know if it's sad or sweet that you think the club will let you go after what happened with Wade. That you think *I'll* let you go after...everything."

"You could help me. You said you love me."

"And you'd go, just like that?" He pulls free of the clenching muscles of my sex and sucks his fingers clean. One by one. All the heat in his eyes is replaced with cold fire.

I can't answer him. I can only watch his face for any sign that he understands how hard all this is to understand.

"This house was supposed to be a refuge for my mother, insulation from the club. It ended up being a prison because there is no escape. I thought maybe..." He shakes his head and brushes a damp finger, still intimately musky, over my cheek. "Doesn't matter what I thought. Cover yourself up.

It's time to head back for the vote. I never should've left in the first place."

SIX

Noah leads me through the club with his hand on the small of my back, possessive but mechanical. I don't dare question him in front of anyone before the vote, but I hate every second of it. I hate that his touch is cold and his jaw is tight. I hate that I can't feel his eyes on me. I hate that this could be the last time I see him.

He drops me in his room back at the club.

"Have a seat." He nudges me toward the bed.

"I..." I'm not sure what I want to say. That I'm sad and angry and scared? That I hate the way his face is a grim mask? That I want him to yell or cuss or do any fucking thing except freeze me out?

He stares at the wall behind me.

"If anyone wants to hear from you during the meeting, a prospect will come and get you like before."

"Anyone? What about you, Noah? Do you want to hear what I have to say?" I seethe through gritted teeth. For the first time in this whole ordeal, I feel like actual luggage. Empty. Property. I watch the muscles in his jaw flex. The slight narrowing of his eyes. He doesn't answer though. The fucker.

"What happens to me if they decide to kill you?"

"Such faith in me." He snarls. "If I'm dead it won't be my problem, will it?"

All the sweet words he'd spoken crash like glass around me. "But—"

"But nothing. You know exactly what'll happen. You're a sweet piece of ass. Someone'll take you." He spits. "And you're just a scared little girl so you'll be happy to be kept."

The door shuts with a quiet, definitive *click.*

"At least slam it, asshole," I shout, balling my fists in the bedspread. Wrapping it around me like armor against Noah's cold disregard, against my memory of gruff bikers crowded around a table deciding his fate.

His fate is supposed to belong to me.

I press my face into the sheets and inhale deeply. Our scents are mingled there—our bodies, the musk of our sex. Sweat, come, tears. It should be disgusting, but it isn't. It's...*us*.

I should've told him I loved him when I had the chance. When his fingers were inside me and we were laughing and dreaming. Before the club got between us. Again. Because this cold, asshole version of Noah, the one who can't seem to muster enough passion to slam the damn door? That bastard is never hearing those three little words cross my lips.

I just hope he lives long enough for me to inform him of this development. But I'm sure as hell not sitting here in the corner like a toddler on the naughty bench, waiting around to find out.

Ella's keys are still on top of Noah's dresser. Her car is still parked out front. I could just...return her car. I did promise to get it back to her. At least it's something useful. And bonus points if Noah worries about me a little while I'm gone.

I snatch the keys and hold my breath. *Please don't be locked. Please don't be locked.* The knob turns without hesitation and I slip out into the dark hallway. I walk with purpose toward the bar. Drew's holding court with a group of women. She waves. "Star, get over here. I got some bitches you need to meet."

My heart clenches. I want to meet them. I do. This is exactly the kind of invitation I'd have hoped for. But I need to hurry the hell up before someone realizes Noah doesn't want me wandering around. "Just gotta grab something out of the car. Be right back."

The lie feels heavy on my tongue. God. They're going to be so scared when I don't come right back. For a second I consider confiding in Drew. She'd been so kind to me that first morning I spent out in the club. She'd understand. Wouldn't she?

"Watch out for the big bad wolf." One of the women calls out.

"Excuse me?"

Drew laughs. "The old lot dog. His name is Wolf. Don't worry. He's all bark, very little bite."

"You'd know all about old dogs, Drew." The same one who'd called to me teases. "I sure as shit hope Zig still bites."

And just like that they're back to their conversation. Smiling and drinking while the whole world could be falling apart. While their men are in a back room deciding Noah's fate. No. I won't tell them anything.

I push through the heavy door and step into the night. Into freedom. Into a cold that settles into my bones almost instantly.

Wolf is nowhere to be seen, though he could be winding through the rows of motorcycles. Dogs freak me out. Mostly because I've never been around them. But I'm a warrior now, and no self-respecting warrior would be afraid of an old dog. I hug myself and pretend I'm not worried.

I get three steps into the parking lot before a gruff voice blasts me from behind. "Where do you think you're going?"

The hand on my shoulder a second later doesn't surprise me. The stench of body odor and a sickly sweet rag against my mouth as soon as I turn to answer does. This is not the wolf they'd warned me about.

SEVEN

My head pounds and my bottom aches. I don't know exactly how long I've been sitting on cold concrete in the musty corner of a basement, but it's long enough for me to have gone numb in places. Dale hadn't bothered to tie me up, so I push myself to my feet and assess my surroundings.

Giant cans of ketchup and pickled beets. Boxes of soda fountain syrup. The safe. I know where I am before I see the big folding table where the cooks and bus boys sometimes get together to play cards. This is the basement of Jimmy's Grill.

Of course. Dale hadn't just been in bed with The Jokers. He'd been in bed with dirty Wade.

That's how Wade had known Noah was busy. How he'd known where to find me.

The wooden stairs leading down from the kitchen above creak under the heavy weight of boots.

"You're a pain in the ass, little girl." Dale calls out from above. "But you're my ticket out of this bullshit. I'm going to trade you for my life. And for a nice chunk of cash to continue that life."

"Noah doesn't give a shit about me. Just the club. I'm worthless." I snap before thinking better of it. My life depends on him thinking I'm valuable.

He spits tobacco juice directly on the floor and pulls a joint out of the front pocket on his shirt. With trembling hands he flicks a lighter, takes a deep drag, and blows a billowing cloud of sweet smoke. "Nothing that belongs to The Devil's Host is worthless."

The truth in his words is not exactly a comfort. I bite my tongue.

"Any minute now they'll be here to collect you and I'll have my walking papers." He blows another smoke cloud and seems to deflate a little, his body relaxing as the pot loosens his muscles. I know that feeling. A little far away. A little floaty. "Just gotta keep everything real chill until then. Just gotta take the edge off."

I don't know if he's telling me that or reassuring himself. While his eyes drift shut as he takes another drag, I scan the area for anything I can use as a weapon. A mop handle. A meat mallet. Anything. There's nothing in my reach except for a gallon jug of bleach. I grab it and hold it out in front of me, unsure of what exactly I might do with it. Hit him? Splash him in the eyes? I'd have to get the cap off for that.

"Easy now, girl. I'm not going to hurt you. As much as I'd like to spend that kind of quality time with you, I think Noah wouldn't feel real generous if I broke his favorite toy."

"I'm not a damn toy. Fuck you, you nasty traitor." My hands are shaking but I somehow manage to get the safety cap screwed off.

Dale laughs. "Want to wash my tighty whiteys? Just ask."

"I'd rather blind you." Then I rush him and swing the jug as hard as I can. Bleach splashes everywhere, the chemical smell stinging my nose, and the heavy plastic container cracks into the side of his skull with a *thunk*. "Or knock you out."

"That was..." Dale takes two wobbly steps backwards and shakes his head. "That was not..."

I don't wait for him to get his bearings back or to finish his thought. I run for the stairs, taking them two at a time, and picking up a splinter in my palm when I forget that the middle section of the railing is rough. I squeeze my hand into a tight ball against the pain, driving the splinter deeper.

The kitchen is dark, but the back door is propped open. I run for that too. And slam into a brick wall on the other side. A leather clad brick wall. Or Noah's chest. Same difference.

"Thank God, you're okay." There's real fear in his voice. And genuine relief. He hauls me up so my feet aren't touching the ground and buries his face in my neck. "I've been so fucking worried. Hours, Star. There were whole goddamn hours where I had no idea where you were or what was happening to you. Un. Fucking. Acceptable."

Stone and two other guys run past us, into the bowels of the restaurant. I don't want to know what they're going to do down there. But I do. They're going to finish what I started. Dale will never fuck with me again. Or the club. I close my eyes and sink into Noah's embrace. The scent of bleach still harsh in my nose.

"I'm okay." I breathe. "You're okay? I was worried about you too." And pissed and hurt. But I don't say any of that. Because this is the Noah I wanted all along. The one who cares. The one who holds me like I'm his heart.

"So worried that you took off?" His tone is annoyed but he doesn't stop squeezing me.

"I wasn't going to go for long. I just wanted to return Ella's car and...let you miss me a little bit." It sounds more ridiculous than I'd imagined. I keep babbling. "You hurt me, Noah. One minute you're melting me from the inside out with sweet words and sweeter touches. The next... ice cold, all business."

He squeezes me tighter still. "You wanted to leave."

"With you, Noah. I wanted to leave with you. That's what I wanted."

He helps me get on the back of his bike, just like the first time. With furtive finger brushes and careful arrangement. "Is that what you still want?" He asks, his voice eerily steady.

I can't answer until he sets the helmet on my head, shielding me from his searching gaze. Blocking out the muffled noises from the basement as Stone, fresh from jail, carries out a death sentence for the club. My words are just barely more than a whisper. And god it hurts to choke them out. "I don't know."

EIGHT

I drive to Ella's in silence, hyper-aware of Noah cruising behind me on his sleek black bike like a horseman of the apocalypse. When he'd agreed to let me return her car I hadn't realized he planned to babysit me. It felt strange but in a good way. He's taking care of me again. And as long as we don't talk about the future, there's none of the eerie calm voice that scares the crap out of me.

I pull up under the carport, careful not to bump the small plastic swimming pool full of tub toys, and hop out to meet up with Noah. Both of us look right at home in front of Ella's trailer with its hardscrabble yard and weathered aluminum siding.

We take the concrete steps together and the screen door of her trailer slams shut behind a tow-headed kid who looks about five or six years old. "Mama, there are strangers at the door."

"Why the hell are you answering the door for strangers?" Ella rounds the corner with an infant on her hip. Her lanky hair is loose around her shoulders, making her look older than the ponytail she always sports at the diner. Or maybe it's the kids. "Star! You're okay?"

"I'm fine." I assure her. "I didn't realize you had a little boy too."

"Oh, yeah. I've actually got four kids but I try not to play that up too much at work. Nobody asks the single mom of four to cover shifts. And I need all the tips I can get. You know how it is." She winces a little. "I'm real glad to see you today though. Jason—my boyfriend—was starting to get...annoyed with me."

There's a shadow around her eye that makes me think Jason does more than get annoyed.

"Thanks for letting me use your car like that. I hope it didn't cause you too much trouble."

"Yeah." She steps through the door and pulls it shut behind her. Then looks left and right, making sure we're alone in the yard. "The cops came by here, Star. I told them I lent my car to my cousin who wanted to audition for a dancing gig in Vegas. I think they bought it but…"

Noah tenses beside me. "But what?"

She brushes her fingers over the bruise and quickly flicks her hair behind her ear as if to mask the movement. ".Jason didn't."

Noah growls. "Did you tell him—"

Ella's face pales and I shove Noah back. "Don't worry about him. Did Jason hurt you because of…because of me?"

"It was my fault, Star. I should've told him right away. I should've warned him there was trouble. He doesn't like surprises."

"God, Ella. I'm so sorry. I'm so so sorry."

"Go pack a bag and get your kids." Noah grunts.

I turn to Noah and place a hand on his chest. "It's not her fault. You don't have to—she won't say anything—she won't—"

"You're god damn right it's not her fault. And there's no way in hell I'm leaving her here to get beat up by some pissant for helping the club." He grabs my chin and looks me in the eyes. His gaze is searing. A host of emotion swirls just beneath the surface—emotions so sweet and true that I'm terrified of them as much as I'm desperate to name them. "For helping you." The last frozen layer around my heart thaws as he turns back to Ella.

233

"If you want protection, you've got it. Is that car in your name?"

Ella nods.

"The trailer?"

"It's a rental."

"Go pack a bag." He says it softer this time but just as firmly. She shifts the baby on her hip and heads back inside.

As soon as she's gone I wrap my arms around him and press my forehead to his chest. "Can you do that? Just take her in?"

"It's been a rough stretch, but the club isn't just about death. I promise. It's a safe place. A family." He plants a rough kiss on the top of my head and laughs. "Are you getting romantic ideas about me again?"

"Maybe."

"Good."

This time the tears soaking his cut are happy ones.

NINE

Settling Ella was easy. She took one look at the filthy floor behind the bar and knocked Drew over to find the cleaning supplies. Settling the kids was even easier. They took one look at this bleak wonderland and let out a whoop of glee. Now I just have to settle Noah.

"They've been playing hard for an hour." I reassure Jules. "I'm sure they won't be any trouble."

"It's fine." Jules says, dropping her sunglasses down from the perch on top of her head. She looks less haunted than she did in the back of Ella's car.

"It's just. I really need to talk to Noah, and I don't want to interrupt Ella while she's getting adjusted."

"Go. Really."

"Are you sure you don't mind watching all these kids?"

"Look, Star. You don't know me so we'll get this straight real quick. If I ever don't want to do something, I promise you there will be zero confusion."

We sit together in silence for a little while. The ancient sandbox behind the club was a surprise. Jules had mentioned family picnics but it'd been hard to picture in the middle of the bar. Out here, I can almost see it. Weeds choke the brick grill, and one of the seats on the old swing set hangs loose, but there'd been something.

"It wasn't always so…desolate out here. Things were different before Dev took over. When my daddy was in charge…" She picks at the fraying edge of the old lawn chair she's sitting on.

I suck in a breath. Their father had been the president? "Why'd Dev take over?"

"Dad got sick. Parkinson's." Jules says it matter-of-factly, but there's a quiver in her lip.

I reach over and squeeze her hand. "But I met him. He's fine. I don't understand."

"Dev took advantage of the situation, but he was within his rights." She shakes her head and drags her toe through the damp sand. "You can't rule if you can't ride. Dad's still got plenty he can do, but it's not safe for him on a bike anymore."

"That's not fair." The words are out of my mouth before I even realize what I'm saying. How naïve I must sound to her. How silly.

It's her turn to squeeze my hand. And let it go. "*Parkinson's* isn't fair. The rules of the club are crystal clear. Things will be different again now that my brother is running the show." She taps my knee. "They already are. You know that."

I find my way back to Noah's room but I barely recognize it. The walls are stripped bare. All the pictures he'd tacked up are crumpled in a trashcan in the corner. "What did you do?"

"I guess I was pretty messed up when I thought you'd left me." He scrubs a hand over his face. "I came out of the vote as president of The Devil's Host and all I wanted to do was tell you. Hold you. Nothing seemed important without you. And you were gone. Walked right out, according to Drew. It was hours before anyone found the ransom note. Hours for me to think about my life. What I wanted. It wasn't any of this bullshit."

"Really?" I can hardly believe the destruction even though I'm looking at it with my own eyes. The passion.

"I'm done collecting debts, baby."

"I know. You're club president now. You'll have someone do that for you."

"It's more than that. I want to be the kind of man that deserves to have you in his life. You asked me to run away with you before. I won't run. That's not who I am. It's not who you are either. But I'll go with you. We can make a life somewhere. Whatever kind of life you want. Two point five fucking kids and a dog named Sparky? Sign me up. I want it all." He steps closer and splays his hand over my belly. "God damn. Just thinking about your belly all big with my babies. Maybe five point five kids."

"Can't we have that here?" I think about his father's sad empty house. Not part of the club. Not part of normal society—whatever that might be—either. And bite my lip.

"If that's what you want." He says it cautiously—quietly. The way you'd talk to a frightened kitten you're trying to lure out of the bushes.

"There's family here, Noah." I think of his father, and Jules, but also of Ella. Of Drew and of Stone. And I think of the babies that are yet to be. Probably not five, though I don't want to tell him that now. "Our family. I want Zig to keep cherries behind the bar for our little ones. I want Stone and your sister to dance at our wedding. I love you. I want to help you lead. Every king needs a warrior queen, right?"

"You love me?"

"How many times do I have to say it?" I echo his words to me. The ones that had melted my heart so thoroughly. "A hundred? A thousand? I will—"

His answering kiss is fast and fierce, knocking the wind from my lungs and bruising my lips. He may only have two arms, but somehow every inch of me feels held. Cherished. Loved. "You love me. Together we can do anything."

TEN

Six months later...

"It's customary for the best man and the maid of honor to dance together after the bride and groom. I swear this is not a conspiracy." I lean against the wall and reach around the corner to thread my fingers with Noah's.

"Fuck if I care. I don't want that filthy biker's hands on my little sister."

"But it's okay for you to put your filthy biker hands on me?"

"Damn right." He tugs, trying to pull me around to his side, but I dig my heels into the courthouse carpet.

"You're not supposed to see me yet."

"Fine." He huffs. "I'll fire him as best man. My father can do the job."

I can't help but smile, imagining his grumpy face. And the black silk bow tie. His tattoos peeking out from beneath French cuffs secured with the tiny silver skull cufflinks I'd gifted him yesterday. The shit-kicking boots polished to a shine to wear with tuxedo pants. "It's too late, Noah. He's already in the ceremony room. With your father. Where you should be. We get married in five minutes."

"Plenty of time for a quickie."

"Not for me."

"Challenge accepted." And just like that, I'm whirling around the corner and over Noah's shoulder.

"Damnit, caveman. They're going to start the wedding march any second."

"Won't get very far without us." He grunts.

A few quick strides away from where we need to be, and one swinging door later, I'm right-side up again. The velour bench beneath me tells me we're in the ladies' room where Drew, Ella, and I had all applied lipstick just a few moments ago. Where I'd told them all how pretty they looked in their little black bridesmaid dresses. "This is so not appropriate."

Noah twists the lock on the door, drops to his knees in front of me, and grins. "Now, I'm going to make you come in less than five minutes. And then I'm going to carry you down the aisle, the taste of you all over my face, and marry the hell out of you. And then I'm going to take a lot longer than five minutes to make you come for the rest of our lives. Forever."

I lean back, accepting my glorious fate. "Is that a threat or a promise?"

He nips my inner thigh in answer. "Both."

I can't think of a more beautiful sight than my lacy skirt in his tattooed hands. Our rings on a chain around his neck.

I tap the ink on his knuckles. "Is this still true? Lost Soul?"

He smiles up at me, over my skirts, his ice blue eyes dancing with wickedness. We've had this conversation so many times. "More than ever. You know I'm lost without you, baby. Now show me what I want to see."

It's easy enough with the scoop neck of my dress. I cup my breasts, lifting them up until they nearly spill out, until the ink over my heart slips into view. It's a delicate work of tangled vines, around the warrior shield of a Viking shield maiden. Beautiful and fierce. The banner across the center is emblazoned with words in the same style as

Noah's knuckles. By the same artist. "Finders Keepers."

I hope you enjoyed The Devil's Host MC Serial. Please consider telling a friend or leaving a review wherever you purchase ebooks. Reviews don't just help authors; they help readers find the books they'll love.

Sign up for my newsletter at sharis-lade.com/newsletter and you'll be the first to know about new releases, giveaways, appearances, and all the fun books I'm busy reading.

I love to hear from readers. You can find me all the places at sharislade.com.

Want more alpha hero hotness right now? Turn the page…

An Extended Excerpt from *Three Nights with a Rock Star* by Shari Slade and Amber Lin

CHAPTER ONE

Friday night

Twenty dollars for parking? Per night. And the garage was the budget-friendly option. Valet didn't even have the price listed. Resigned, Hailey dug in her purse for a twenty and handed it over. The booth attendant raised his eyebrow, giving her car a once-over. Well, okay. Message received. She clearly didn't belong at the ritzy hotel, even as a visitor.

It was true. She normally spent less than twenty dollars a day on food. And her old Toyota had broken down twice on the drive into Chicago. Heck, the booth attendant probably made more than she did. But if she was going to be stuck here for a few days, she'd have to adjust her standards a little bit. It was for a good cause.

A necessary cause.

The garage was filled to the brim, a gleaming array of BMWs, Porsches, and other brands she couldn't name. They looked like jewels on a velvet display case, her rusty hunk of steel an unseemly contrast.

She traveled lower, into the bowels of the hotel, and found an open space hiding in a corner. Her coupe managed to squeeze between the painted concrete wall and the metal Dumpster. She wrinkled her nose at the smell already seeping inside the car.

Holding her breath, she peeked at herself in the rearview mirror.

A stranger stared back at her. A stranger with heavy eyeliner and blue shadow. And glitter all over her face. The eye makeup had been on purpose. The glitter had been an unfortunate accident with the shimmer powder and a stuck lid.

She hadn't bothered to wash it off, though. It made her look fun and zany, like the kind of person who would take a dare and up the stakes. The kind of person who would crash a major label band's after-party. It made her look like a different person, and for the next few days that was who she would be.

Focus. She could do this. She *had* to do this.

The car door clattered against the metal wall of the Dumpster, leaving only a sliver of space. She sucked in her stomach and squeezed through—and heard an unfortunate rip. *Damn.* She glanced down. She'd torn her stockings. Her sister's stockings, technically.

Hailey was used to getting runs in her stockings at work. Chubby little hands with razor-sharp nails made it common. But this was more than a small run. This was a gaping hole right at her left ankle. Hazards of wearing fishnets, she supposed.

It seemed colder here even though the temperature shouldn't be much different than Lake Elkhart. Maybe it was the lack of blood circulation after driving for hours . Or maybe it was nerves. Either way, she felt chilled to the bone. She reached inside for the cardigan she always left stashed in her backseat. It never hurt to be prepared.

She followed the signs to the elevator bay, breathing a sigh of relief as she cleared the Dumpster's smelly radius. The button lit red while she waited.

Ding.

She wobbled as she moved in front of the elevator about to open. How did her sister wear these shoes, anyway? Reflective gold doors slid apart, revealing a couple. Having sex. Or almost having sex? She wasn't sure. But the rhythmic motions and clothes shoved aside certainly indicated…good Lord.

Their harsh breathing echoed in the elevator. They were moving, rubbing, grinding. A flash of pink skin. Hailey definitely shouldn't have seen anything pink, but she couldn't stop looking.

246

Couldn't stop staring. Her eyelids were frozen, her whole body clamped into place, pinned under the weight of her own naïveté.

The guy looked up from the elevator floor. His heated gaze ran down her body and up again, and unlike the booth attendant, this guy seemed pleased with what he saw.

Her mouth hung open. She snapped it shut.

"Pardon me," she said inanely. As if *she* had been the one to interrupt them. Which, in a way, she had been.

His grin was feral. "Come on in. Water's fine."

Oh my God. "No, thank you. I'll catch the next one."

Of its own volition, her gaze wandered down the slope of his back to the guy's exposed ass, clenching and thrusting. She wasn't about to join in, but in some distant, terrifying way, the scene tugged at her.

The girl beneath him giggled as she watched Hailey from beneath heavy lids. "He calls it a joyride."

"I can see why," Hailey said faintly.

The elevator doors closed on their laughter. She stared at her own reflection once again. The elevator bay echoed silent, absent of gasped breaths and fabric rubbing against fabric.

So, that was different.

She took a deep breath of cool, stale air.

On the upside, she now felt totally awake after her long, drowsy drive. Way more effective than a jolt of caffeine could have been. Half-naked people rutting on the elevator floor were her own personal splash of water in the face.

On the downside, she wasn't sure she could pull off her plan anymore. She wasn't cut out for this. This was Chloe's scene. Chloe wouldn't have been freaked out by a couple having a good time. Though Hailey had no desire to imagine her sister going on a *joyride.*

Remembering her reaction, her stomach sank. *No, thank you.* Ugh. Could she be any more prim? She'd just been…shocked. Had she *ever* seen two other people having sex before? No. In real life, no. There had been a few wayward Internet searches she wasn't entirely sure were proper.

She stood in the musty alcove, torn by indecision. Should she still go up? What choice did she have?

Her phone beeped. She glanced at the screen to see a text from Chloe.

Pineapple and canadian bacon?

Her heart panged. It was a peace offering, that text. Things had been strained between them the past few days, after her sister's revelation. They had always been best friends or mortal enemies,

THE DEVIL'S HOST MC

constantly teasing or at each other's throats, so the quiet politeness had been unnerving.

The text also meant her sister hadn't found the quickly scrawled note letting her know that Hailey would be gone for a few days. The pizza delivery and C-rated movie would have to wait until she got back.

One good thing: the exchange steeled her resolve. Her spine straightened. She pressed the elevator button again and texted back for Chloe to eat without her.

She was doing this for her sister. Her only family. She needed to do it, or everything she'd worked toward in taking care of Chloe, in building a better life for them, would be for nothing. She had to, or history would repeat itself.

So when the reflective doors opened again, she stepped into the elevator. Stepped through the looking glass, where everything was upside-down and inside out, and so was she.

What she found was...disaster.

Hailey had imagined her arrival in the hotel several times during the long drive over. In her mind it would be more like storming a castle than pushing through heavy glass doors. In every fantasy she had been tough. Even fierce.

In none of them had she stumbled over a stranger who was halfway to puking into a lobby fern. And then he *was* puking. There were a few other people sprawled on couches or just right on the floor, but no one looked conscious. And certainly no one looked concerned by the sick man at her feet.

She knelt and awkwardly patted his back. He listed to the side and landed with his head in her lap.

Ugh. She fished in her purse for a wet wipe and pressed it into his hand. Those wipes always came in handy for runny noses or sticky hands. With a sleepy burp the man in her arms closed his eyes and appeared to fall asleep.

Should she...just leave him here?

That seemed wrong. But then again, he was hardly alone. There were a multitude of sleeping— or stoned?—bodies strewn around the sleek, modern lobby. It seemed a little early to have partied and collapsed by seven p.m., like they were her preschoolers who were wild all day and then crashed at a reasonable bedtime.

Despite the hefty price tag that surely accompanied such a place, no attendant stood behind the glass-paneled counter. A swanky hotel like this one would have someone stationed all night long. Maybe they had fled the scene.

Maybe Hailey would be smart to follow suit.

But she couldn't leave. She hadn't spent the last ten years taking care of her sister only to mess it up now. Arguably she already *had* messed it up, but she was going to fix it. She wouldn't leave until it was fixed. She just had to find the lead singer— he went by the name of Lock—and appeal to his better nature...but first she had to figure out what to do with the passed-out guy in her lap.

From the wispy shadows down a corridor came the squeak of steps. At least someone here was awake and upright. And tall, she realized, listening to the slow, casual pace. Hopefully he would know where she could find Lock.

CHAPTER TWO

Lock stormed into the lobby. Moe had ganked and he was going to get it back. Even if it meant wading through the pile of half-naked bodies spread before him. The air was thick with sweat, bong water, bourbon, and vomit. His stomach should turn, but all he wanted to do was roll around in it. Like a stray dog.

No. He might be dirty, but he'd been sober for 372 days. Screwing that up was not an option.

His career—his life—depended on it. He knew too well how one misstep could destroy everything. He had the sex tape, the canceled tour dates and now the record label's sword of Damocles hanging over his head to prove it.

He tripped over Krist, who was sprawled on the floor in front of an empty upholstered chair, like he'd shot for the seat and given up a few steps short. His face pressed into the hotel lobby carpet, muffling his words. "The fuck, man?"

"Looking for Moe. You know where he landed?"

"Up some redhead's skirt." Krist rolled onto his back, exposing his inked stomach—the cover art from their first album—and the top of his junk. His pants were still open.

Lock nudged him in the ribs with his boot. "Zip it, man. And roll over. We don't need you pulling a Hendrix."

"Whatever, *bro*. You flashed your shit all over the Internet."

He winced. *Bro* was a reference to the weeklong hookup between Lock's mother and Krist's father in the endless '80s rock-star sex parade. They weren't really siblings—in fact, far from it. But they used the name as a reminder of their shared past. They'd both been castoffs on tour. Too young to party but old enough to want to. They'd picked up guitars and taught themselves—taught each other—to play. Screwing around with instruments they had no business touching. *Some things never change.* Krist hadn't called him *bro* in a long time. Not since before Lock had started fucking everything up, long before he'd *flashed his shit*. He hadn't chosen to do that. Someone had done it for him. But he'd owned it like it was all part of his master plan. What else was he supposed to do? *Bro.* It was a stalemate. The cold war within the Half-Life band.

He nudged Krist again. "I mean it, *bro*."

Krist flipped him off but rolled over anyway. Lock wasn't in charge, but people usually did what he said. Usually. Since he'd—what did his agent call it?—*embraced sobriety*. Not fucking Moe.

253

Where was that sneaky bastard? Lock wanted to embrace his balls with a vise.

The formerly gorgeous lobby was a pit. The label was going to bill them a fortune for this shit. And piss their pants with excitement. *Half-Life Bad Boys Trash Hotel, Orgy in Chicago Hilton.* Those headlines sold concert tickets. Sex, drugs and rock and roll, baby.

As long as *he* wasn't doing it. As long as it didn't go too far. They wanted the *illusion* of debauchery. The other guys could hold it together. For now. All Lock did was fall apart.

He followed the sound of dry heaves, and there was Moe. Cradled in the arms of some blonde who was rubbing his back. Was she humming a fucking lullaby?

"You're not a redhead." She wasn't. She wasn't a groupie either. Groupies did not wear cardigans to hotel parties. Smoky shadow rimmed her eyes, but she still somehow looked like a Sunday school teacher sitting right in the middle of hell.

"Not the last time I checked." She shrugged and kept rubbing Moe's back. Definitely not a groupie. A groupie would've recognized him and dumped Moe like last week's trash. Unless she had a thing for drummers. It happened. That's all they were— fetishes that could be tried and discarded before the girls returned to the nice guys back home.

He gave her a lazy perusal. "What are you doing here?"

I was hoping to meet L-Lock. Do you know where I could find him?" Her pink lips quirked into a wide smile. False bravado. He knew that when he saw it too.

This might be entertaining. He pushed up the sleeve of his shirt, exposing his most photographed tattoo, a serpent coiled around an anatomical heart. She couldn't miss it. "You a big fan?"

"Oh, yeah. Really big fan."

She was lying. And sober. Who sat in the middle of this mess sober? She could be some weird star fucker, looking to hook up with anyone famous just to say she did. *That can be arranged.* Though she wouldn't be telling anyone, not after she signed his agreement. Not without paying a hefty penalty and having her name raked through the tabloids.

He forced a wide yawn, flashing his trademark tongue stud. No recognition. Maybe she didn't worship at his alter; she just worshipped celebrity. Worship. She looked like her kind of worship involved hymnals and psalms.

A flash of her on her knees—*not in prayer*—made him waver. This might be more than entertaining; it might be fun. It had been a long time since he'd had fun.

"I can take you to him. If you're not too busy." He waved his hand at Moe, his lucky guitar pick all but forgotten.

"Help me with him?" She tried to force Moe from her lap, but he was 200 pounds of uncooperative asshole. Lock grabbed his drummer by the shoulders and lifted his upper body away from...the church mouse. She was probably a Penelope or a Polly. Pure.

"What's your name?"

"Hailey. Thanks. I wasn't expecting to find everyone crashed already. Do you always party until you puke by seven p.m.?" She pulled something out of her purse. A wet nap? And turned around to bend over Moe.

Without a lump of drummer covering half her body, he was shocked to find black fishnets covering her legs. And a short denim skirt barely covering her ass. None of it suited her.

A costume.

"Didn't you hear, fan girl? The new single went platinum today. They started celebrating at noon. Anyone can party at midnight, it takes a real rock star to get it done in the daylight. Besides, this is half-time. They'll rally for another round."

"Oh," she said faintly. Then she wiped Moe's mouth and rolled him onto his side. Who was this chick?

He held out his hand, intrigued. Would she break character first or would he? "Follow me, Hailey. Let me lead you down into the belly of the beast."

And then he knew, without a doubt, she wasn't a groupie. That lyric. A real groupie would've come on the spot, right in her fucking panties. He couldn't count how many times random fan girls begged him, *Say it say it say it.* He never did. Why the hell had he said it now?

CHAPTER THREE

Hailey followed him down the hallway he'd come from. *Into the belly of the beast,* she thought with amusement. It had been hard to suppress her smile when he'd first said the words. She'd heard the phrase used ironically, of course, but he'd been heartbreakingly serious. And he had watched so carefully for her reaction. Luckily she had years of experience with preschoolers telling her all sorts of wild things. She knew how to keep a straight face.

"What did you say your name was?" she asked.

He stopped abruptly and turned, eyes narrowed.

She stumbled and barely avoided running into him. Her breath caught. It struck her suddenly how close their faces were. He was tall, and so was she on these ridiculous platform heels she'd borrowed from her sister. This close, she could see silver in the dusting of dark scruff along his jaw, even though he looked closer to her age. It seemed to suit him. He was metallic all over, from the tiny flecks of gold in his eyes to the sleek onyx ink tattooed on his arm.

And the peek of a silver piercing in his tongue when he spoke.

She'd never known a tongue piercing could be sexy. She wasn't sure why it was sexy now either, except that it just hinted at so much...sensual knowledge. And she'd always had a yearning for knowledge.

"I didn't," he said curtly, responding to her question. But when he continued forward, he spoke without looking at her. "You can call me Keaton."

"Oh," she said, somewhat breathless as she hurried to catch up.

The heels made her wobble like a newborn fawn, gangly and uncertain on her legs. He noticed, she knew, glancing back ever so slightly as he walked, lashes veiling his eyes. Though he was kind enough not to comment. And kind enough to take her to Lock without asking too many questions. A kind man, then.

She felt a sort of kinship with him, with *Keaton*. He was the only one here, besides her, who was fully clothed and sober. She, too, was used to being the responsible one. The one slightly apart from the rest.

Maybe it was presumptuous to think she could relate to a man who wore the rock-and-roll trappings like a second skin. But she knew as well as anyone that clothes were just camouflage. She'd had to sneak this entire outfit from her sister's closet, since her preference for pastels would hardly fit in here.

He stopped in front of an elevator and swiped his hotel key card. The doors opened immediately.

At least no writhing bodies met her sight. Even the memory of them made her cheeks heat.

Keaton held the door and gestured her inside the empty elevator, the movement faintly mocking. Inside, the carpet tilted her heels every which way, and she clung to the gilded railing as he pressed the button for the top floor.

The penthouse. Of course Lock would be staying in the best room. And of course Chloe would be awed by such glamour.

No, she was being unfair. Chloe had obsessed over Lock and the entire band for years. So when she'd secured the summer gig selling merchandise—or as Chloe called it, merch—on their tour, Hailey had tried to be happy for her sister, she really had. Even though it meant forgoing the extra summer classes they'd planned so Chloe could finish college sooner. Even though she called for Hailey to wire her money after a particular incident with a vending machine thrown out a window.

Even when Chloe came home pregnant.

God, even then Hailey had pasted on a smile. This was a *blessing*. She was almost sure about that. She would *make* it a blessing. But then, the final straw. The father wasn't going to be involved. He wasn't even going to help, not financially, not emotionally. He wanted no part of the child's life. And Chloe wouldn't tell her who the father was.

She wanted to let the whole thing drop, when she and Hailey had been raised without a father and hardly a mother either, and they knew how painful it was. How desolate.

Hailey wasn't going to let that happen.

The elevator gave a muted *ding,* and the doors slid open. Directly into someone's living room. The kind of opulent, expansive place Hailey had only ever pictured on the glossy pages of a magazine. She hadn't even *bought* the magazine. She'd flipped through it in line at the grocery store and then guiltily returned it before checkout because who had $3.99 to spend on envy? But this was the real thing.

Like the half-naked bodies in the elevator—no longer pictures but the real thing.

She forced herself inside, hovering near the elevator even as it shut behind her.

Keaton showed no such hesitation. He strolled in like he'd been here a thousand times before. She supposed, since Lock trusted him with a key card, he probably had. Maybe he was an assistant of some kind. He went to a large bar and popped the lid of a Coke. No vending machines for penthouse residents.

He cocked the bottle toward her. "You want one?"

She shook her head, taking a hesitant step forward. "Do you know when Lock will be here?"

He sprawled into a large leather chair, one leg over the square arm, and took a sip of his drink. Chicago's twinkling nightscape framed him from behind. He looked so incongruously regal, sitting there, like a king surveying all he owned. And she knew, with a sinking feeling, what he was going to say before he did.

"Sweetheart, you're looking at him."

***

Her shoulders slumped, and her mouth settled into a disconcerting line of determination. The look on her face. She looked...resigned. He'd wanted to shock her, to watch her fluster and backpedal.

"Not what you expected?" he asked.

"No, you're exactly what I expected. I don't know why I didn't realize sooner. It's not like I've never seen your picture. I'm a little embarrassed. Do you mind if I sit?"

He nodded, still intrigued. She didn't lie or try to make herself look better. She just told the truth. What else might she say?

Her gaze darted around the room, a mouse scanning for danger, and she settled on the edge of a chaise lounge across from him. Then she took off her shoes—actually took off her shoes—and rubbed her stockinged feet. Worked her thumb deep into the arch, sighing. He felt it in his groin.

"Gosh, my feet hurt. I don't know how my sister wears these things. If I put anything other than a sneaker or a croc near my toes, they just curl up in terror. Like the Wicked Witch of the East. Taking off my shoes is my favorite part of the day. That and my bra. Oh."

"By all means, take that off too."

She bit her lip and flushed. He knew she regretted that last admission as soon as it was out of her pretty mouth. She didn't look like the kind of girl who discussed her underwear in mixed company, but he couldn't resist pushing. This nervous babble was getting more interesting by the minute. The tantalizing peek of her bare toes through the fishnet was getting more interesting too.

He watched her school her features, bring herself back to calm and dignity. It was so much like what he did before he went onstage. Only in reverse. She steadied; he frenzied.

She took a deep breath. "I'd appreciate it if you didn't tease me. It isn't nice."

Her quiet reprimand brought him up short. No one had expected niceness from him, ever. He'd grown up on tour with his parents, rock royalty who'd lived fast and died not quite as young as they'd expected. He'd been treated alternately like a tiny king and luggage. He'd had almost everything he wanted and nothing he needed. He wouldn't know where to begin...being nice. "I'm not teasing. I'm being a good host. Seeing to your comfort. I'll even take it off for you."

She shook her head like he'd offered her another unwanted soda. So she wasn't here to try and fuck him. Why did that make his dick hard?

"I have a problem—a private, family matter—and I'd like your help."

He leaned back in the chair, inhaling the leathery scent, and rubbed his eyes. Of course she wanted something. A signed photograph? A vial of some bodily fluid? A sweaty T-shirt worn onstage? Exhaustion settled over him like a lead blanket. "What do you want?"

"Last month you bought my sister a bus ticket home. She toured with you this summer. She's..."

"She's what? Sorry she left? If she got a ticket home, it's because she needed to leave. I doubt she'd be welcome back, even if you do plead her case. And I don't buy tickets. Our tour manager might."

"She's pregnant."

So it was *that* scam again. This was part of the reason he had his agreement. No questionable paternity suits for him. Not anymore. He knew exactly who he fucked, when, and for how long. He had them stored in a file, and since he hadn't added to that in file nine months, he knew it wasn't this girl's transient sister. "Not by me. Not my problem."

"I didn't say it was yours. I'm pretty sure it isn't, because she won't talk about the father. She'd be shouting it from the rooftops if it was you. You're a god in her eyes."

"I'm no god. A demon, maybe." Keeping starry-eyed groupies from broadcasting his conquests was another reason for his agreement. Too often their excitement turned sour, the fantasy never quite matching the reality. Turned out he didn't magically become one of their nice guys when they fucked him, like some frog getting kissed. He'd written "Scorned" after a particularly grueling bout of tabloid vengeance.

Her soft brown eyes raked over his body. He could almost feel her gaze searching for scales and a tail. So fucking earnest. He wished he could sprout horns on the spot, to make her sad smile falter. "I was hoping you'd be able to help me find the father."

Now he was shocked. "You want me to interview my band? My crew? Pass her picture around at sound check? That isn't how it works."

"Nothing like that. We don't want it public. We both work for our church, and a scandal would be awful."

"Church?" He nearly snorted his soda, the bubbles tickling the back of his throat. "I'm surprised you didn't burst into flames downstairs. What do you do at church? No, let me guess. Sunday school?"

She pursed her lips. "Well yes. But that's volunteer work. Chloe volunteers with the youth group. My paid job is in the attached child-care center."

Of course. Another person paid to care. Worried about her job. "I can see why you'd want to keep this quiet."

"I think if I can talk to some of the people here, I might be able to figure it out. Quietly. I could blend in? Like a groupie? Just for a few days. So I can convince him to do the right thing."

A few days to ask around and figure out who her sister had fucked. Without it becoming public knowledge. Un-freaking-likely. Her plan was as thin as the air in the nosebleeds at Madison Square Garden, and judging from the desperation in her eyes, she knew it. But family could drive people to crazy depths; he knew all about that. For that and many reasons, he should throw her out, maybe even call the cops. This had stalker written all over it, but he couldn't hold back the grin spreading across his face as it clicked in his mind, exactly what he was going to do. He had so few vices left. "Stand up. Let me look at you."

She rose slowly. "Maybe I will take that drink. What do people drink when they have no idea what they're doing? Beer? Tequila?"

"Beer is for barbecue. Tequila is for bad decisions. And whiskey is for all-purpose adjustment. It's what I always reached for when I drank. But I can't help you drown your troubles in booze. Or are you looking for liquid courage?"

"No, I just—" The jut of her chin told him courage was exactly what she'd been looking for. He cast a glance at the bar, cleared of all alcoholic beverages prior to his arrival per his agent's instructions. Not even a bottle of bitters. Like he'd ever been that desperate.

"You won't find a drop of that here. I can call downstairs—"

"No, it's fine. It's not like I'm really a drinker." She shivered. "I hate the taste."

He regretted ever acquiring it.

She'd never pass as a groupie. Not even with her ripped fishnets and glitter fetish. She'd looked too horrified, too out of place in the middle of all the debauchery downstairs. And tonight was tame. But if she was with him? How badly did she want this particular all-access pass?

"You can stay, but I'll need you to agree to a few terms first."

"Whatever you want."

"Yes, that's number one on the list."

***

Hailey forced herself to stand still for his leisurely perusal. Even when he stood and stalked toward whatever dregs she had left after donning these clothes and almost falling on her face. But his smile hit her like a blast of heat, blinding her, scalding her. He looked far too pleased with himself, like a man about to get everything he wanted. And her shaky insides warned she might just give it to him.

"What do you mean?" she asked, proud her voice didn't quaver too much.

"You want to stay here while we're in Chicago," he said. "To stay here for three days, to blend in so that no one questions why you're here. To ask questions, poke around."

Yes, that was exactly what she wanted. So why did her nod feel like surrender? As if she'd agreed to his terms before she even knew them. But then maybe she *did* know what his terms would be. His eyes spoke the words his lips had yet to say. There were volumes of gold-flecked pages filled with all that sensual knowledge. They promised delight and, even better, a hard bite to the exchange. Where the men she had been with were a fresh spring breeze, he stood before her like the calm before the storm, his eyes darkening clouds.

"Can you..." She licked her lips. His gaze tracked the movement, making her feel hunted. "Can you help me?"

His expression softened. Just the slightest degree, but it was enough to slow the hammering of her heart. This was the same kind man she'd met in the lobby. Desire had given him a rough edge, turning his loping gait into a prowl, making his scenting her. But he was still kind inside.

When he didn't answer, she searched for whatever strength she might have found. *You want...* he'd said, listing *her* terms. Only *his* terms were left to be stated. A negotiation, then. But even as she thought the words, an image flashed through her mind, a gazelle caught from behind, the vicious beauty of her captor feasting in a *National Geographic* special.

"What do you want?" she whispered, and somehow the wall was at her back. He was at her front...crowding her...embracing her?

"You," he snarled. "Under me. Over me. On your knees in front of me. I get full artistic license to your body for three days."

His words pounded her like hail, leaving dents and then pooling in the hollows left behind. They drowned out the rest of the world and shook the but her gaze remained locked with his. The shaking was on the inside, fear and a strange longing warring inside her, a battle to the death. She stood frozen, caught in his sights and too terrified to run. Too curious to walk away.

He stepped back, sending a wash of crisp hotel air over her body. She sucked in a breath and immediately missed the earthy scent of him.

"And you," he continued conversationally, "will have total access to play Nancy Drew in the hotel. That is, whenever I'm not using you."

Her body lit up when he said the word *using*. It imploded on *you*, spoken with such self-assured possession. What was wrong with her that she wanted to be used? Maybe because she wanted to be free to enjoy sex, to really explore it, for the first time in her tame little life. Maybe because *he* would be the one using her, and he seemed like he would know just what to do with her.

This was a bad idea. For reasons that weren't quite coming to her at the moment. But she knew it was bad. If she'd said it once, she'd said it a thousand times to her preschoolers: don't make decisions when you're angry. Though she wasn't angry. She was concerned. And frustrated. And…

God, Chloe, why? After I worked so freaking hard so you could start college, why couldn't you be more careful?

Okay, she might be angry.

She swallowed. So maybe this weekend could be for her too. She *would* find the baby's father, but she'd also find something for herself.

With a deep breath, she struggled for levity. A lopsided tilt of her lips was all she could manage. "Where do I sign?" she joked.

His grin widened, revealing an even row of white teeth. The Cheshire cat had just such a smile. "I'm so glad you asked. I have blank copies of my contract in the side table. Right next to the lube."

CHAPTER FOUR

Chloe stared at the white oval, willing a second blue line not to appear. It did. Just like it had for the last seven strips. She'd also been disappointed by a red circle, a pink plus, and the word *Not* never forming in front of the word *Pregnant*.

She tossed the current plastic stick into the little trash can overflowing with cardboard packaging and instructions. Stupid. She was stupid for taking so many tests, as if they could all be wrong, as if the doctor's office could have been wrong.

It was just like when her mother left behind that hastily scrawled phone number. Chloe had called the number again and again. Even when Hailey shook her head and said Mom wasn't coming back, Chloe had waited until her sister went to sleep and then dialed the number so many times she could hear the disconnected chime in her dreams. Her sister had always been smarter.

Getting pregnant at nineteen was stupid too, but Chloe couldn't think about that right now. She was still here, in this place of uncertainty and possibilities. The *maybe I'm somehow not pregnant* possibility.

But she was. She'd known it since she missed her first period while on tour with Half-Life. She'd felt something, *someone* inside her, even though the

Internet claimed it was too soon to know. In denial, she'd packed up and boarded a Greyhound without even sending so much as a text to...well, without telling a soul.

Sitting on the toilet, she put her head in her hands.

Options. She needed to consider her options. There should be a flowchart for this situation that asked you questions and led you to the right answer.

At the very top it would ask, *What would you say if a cute guy offers to teach you guitar?* Yes.

If he plays you a song about love lost and then kisses you, what then?

If you're both drunk on lust, and he just wants to see what it would be like, just wants to feel you without anything between you, would you do it?

But she couldn't blame it on him. She'd wanted to feel him too, and it had felt insanely good, impossibly sweet, like for the first time she wasn't having sex, she was making love. He'd pulled out, but not soon enough, obviously.

Stupid.

She sighed. The next rectangle in the flowchart would ask, *Did you get pregnant?* And yes, she had. She could admit that now, after using up an entire shelf at the drugstore.

Next box in the chart. *Do you want an abortion?* No, not when she already *felt* the little alien inside her. *Adoption?* Better, but she wasn't sure about that either. Her mother had left them, but Chloe had been okay because she had Hailey. Hailey to make sure she did her homework and Hailey to set her curfew. Hailey to hold her when she came home crying because she was pregnant. She couldn't be sure her child would have that. And she refused to make Hailey be a mother to another child she hadn't given birth to. So, the only person Chloe could count on to be a mother to this child was herself.

She *wanted* to be a good mother to her child. Strange but true.

All she had to do, then, was figure out how to be Hailey.

Where was her sister anyway? *Weren't you just saying you'd rely on yourself, not her?* Okay, but still, it was weird. The ever-responsible Hailey had disappeared without telling Chloe where she'd gone.

Chloe left the bathroom and stood in the open doorway to Hailey's empty room as if it might hold a clue, as if a brochure to Tahiti might have been left on the nightstand. Maybe with the tagline *Stressed because your baby sister got herself knocked up? Well, come on down to our resort and relax.* Chloe wouldn't even blame her.

But it was weird.

The bed was made. Of course. The nightstand was clear of everything except a book her sister had been reading, with its pages dog-eared. The closet looked undisturbed, with not enough missing to really suggest a long trip. Even those sensible green crocs were in their proper cubby. Hailey loved those crocs.

Chloe pulled her phone from her pocket and found her sister's name. *Seriously, where are you?*

A few minutes later the response came. *I told you, I'm fine. Don't worry.*

Well of course she was fine. This was Hailey, who always had her shit together, who always did the right thing. But it didn't really answer the question. Where the hell was she?

A little bubble on the screen indicated she had other text messages from someone else. She didn't want to look. She wasn't going to look.

She looked.

Hey, I heard you left the tour
Did something happen? Are you okay?
Call me

She winced. Fuck. She could just imagine his expression too, a mixture of frustration and concern. She hadn't even been sure he cared about her when she left. Maybe she'd just been a convenient lay.

She was used to being a convenient lay, really.

Between the guys at her high school and the random hookups at concerts, it had been a leapfrog game of sex that she'd found exciting at first. And then just tiring. Except for him. He'd been...something different. Something real, until she'd gotten scared and split.

She texted back: *I'm okay. Call you soon.* And then shut off her phone. Which was cowardly, but that was what he got for dealing with the irresponsible sister. Anyway, she would tell him. She'd have to.

Tonight maybe.

With a final, fruitless glance, she left her sister's bedroom and went into her own. She was ready to fall onto the bed and possibly hide under the covers for the next nine months when something from the closet caught her eye.

Unlike Hailey's tidy closet, Chloe's was overflowing with clothes and bling. Satiny halter tops and a tiara. Heavy metal T-shirts and Mardi Gras beads. She kept most of her clothes for clubbing near the back. She just bunched them into a ball and threw them into a Rainbow Brite bucket. Except now they were all rolled into little symmetrical piles, and there was only one person who could fold fishnet stockings that neatly.

What the hell had Hailey been doing in her closet? They'd agreed never to cross each other's thresholds, as if they were state lines and violation an act of war. Sure Chloe still secretly borrowed clothes occasionally, like that cardigan when she'd been Sandra Dee for Halloween. But Hailey never even wore clothes like Chloe's, especially not the party stuff. It didn't make sense.

She picked through all her clothes and found her platform boots missing. Her stilettos too. God, Hailey would break an ankle in those. Chloe almost had several times. Her slinky black dress was gone. A few tops. Possibly a pair of acid-washed jeans.

She sat amid the textile wreckage and shook her head. The world was turning upside down. Here she was at home alone on a Friday night. Hailey was out someplace mysterious, past curfew. Well, one thing was for sure, wherever her sister was, she was looking damn hot.

And Chloe knew where she needed to go.

***

Hailey sat at the gleaming dining room table, alone in the expansive room. She bit her lip and stared at her sister's smiling pic on the phone screen. She had avoided calling Chloe on the way here, knowing it would change her mind. But the text messages and voice mails had already started coming. If Hailey didn't answer for the whole weekend—the full three days of the contract—Chloe would genuinely worry.

With a sigh, Hailey pressed the Call button.

Her sister sounded cautious. "Did you get lost picking up a movie?"

"No, I...I forgot about movie night." She grimaced. As explanations went, that one was weak.

There was a weighted silence. "You mean the movie night we've had every Friday for three years. *That* movie night?"

"Except for when you were gone on tour," Hailey retorted, but it was a cheap shot. Her sister was *pregnant,* for God's sake. Hailey should be there, making sure she was comfortable, making sure she ate enough.

And she would...right after this.

This was for the best. This was *necessary.* She had to believe that, because the alternative felt too much like history repeating itself. Absent parents and struggling to get by. No, Hailey wouldn't let that happen.

She'd just have to say it quickly, like tearing off a Band-Aid. "I'm in Chicago. At the hotel where the band is staying."

"*What?*"

"I know you said to drop it, that the father wasn't interested and you're fine with that, but *I'm* not fine with that. It's not right for the baby to grow up without a father."

"You realize this is the twenty-first century, right? There are women who have babies alone on purpose."

"Well, you aren't one of them. And those women probably have careers and…you know, money. They aren't nineteen years old and dropping out of college, with no plan for their life."

A huff of breath. "No, tell me how you really feel. I can take it."

Her stomach twisted with guilt. "I'm sorry. I didn't mean it like that." That sounded lame, so she added, "You know I love you."

God, how could that sound lamer?

"I love you too," Chloe said with that pouting voice, which helped strengthen Hailey's resolve. Chloe was practically a baby. And now she was having a baby. *Someone* had to do *something,* and this desperate race over Illinois's plains was the only plan she'd come up with at five p.m. today.

"Look, just tell me who the father is, and I'll talk some sense into him."

"I can't believe you're even in Chicago. Who are you, and what you have done with my sister?"

"Even if he doesn't want to be involved with the child—after I've talked to him—he has a financial obligation. We should talk to a lawyer."

"That's definitely not happening."

"Chloe, this isn't money for you or me. This is money for the child."

"Can you please stop saying *the child* the same way you'd say *the plague* or *Voldemort*. He can hear you, you know."

"No, he can't—" Hailey let out an exasperated sound because Chloe was just messing with her. That was Chloe, always casual, always chill. But this whole situation? Not casual. And Hailey was feeling a long way from chill.

"Tell me his name," Hailey said sternly. It was her *mom voice*, as Chloe called it. Usually right before she said the words...

"You can't make me."

"I'm going to find him anyway. You're just making this harder."

"No, I'm making it *impossible*. As it should be. You're never going to find him."

It felt like a challenge. Was it supposed to feel like a challenge? Did Chloe secretly want her to find the father and convince him to help? Regardless, it was happening. Starting with this contract, which would give her the access she needed. Not to mention a place to stay in the swanky hotel that was probably booked solid.

"I'm going to find out who the father is," she said softly. Fiercely. "And he's going to help."

That definitely came out like a challenge. Hailey didn't *want* this to be a sibling-rivalry thing, but maybe it was too late for that. No matter how many times she'd said *do your homework* or *please don't graffiti our living room wall*, she was still a sister. Not a parent.

Chloe sighed. "Oh, Sis. I love that you want to help me. I just hate the way you're doing it."

Hailey swallowed hard as she stared down at the printed sheets of paper in front of her. This was her own personal gauntlet, walking on the fire of her secret desires. She'd have to give Lock whatever he wanted—and get what she wanted in return. She hated it too. But she also kind of loved it.

"I'll be home in a couple of days," Hailey said. "In the meantime, make sure you eat enough. And go to sleep early."

Chloe snorted. "In your dreams."

Somewhat reassured, Hailey ended the call. At least that much was the same between them. Because so much else had changed. On a typical Friday night Hailey would be throwing popcorn at Chloe while her sister chatted through the movie. She'd read two chapters of her library book and go to sleep by eleven. Whereas today...what *was* she doing? It was hard to tell, even with the words spelled out in black-and-white. The gleaming sheets of paper with crisp ink might as well have been a crumbling stone wall painted with hieroglyphs. Strings of symbols her mind couldn't comprehend.

Confidentiality Agreement, it said in bold letters at the top. And right here, she had to come to terms with the fact that he'd been serious about the contract. A real piece of paper, signed by both parties and filed...where? The Department of Rock-Star Relations? The Ministry of the Rich and Famous?

But farther down the words grew stranger. Her brain turned to mush, unable to process the bluntness of *bodily available* and *kink allowances.* She had, in the heat of the moment, agreed to do anything with him. Anything *for* him. But both her arousal and impulsiveness had deserted her now. She shuddered under the draft of air-conditioning above the desk.

Most of the contract was in legalese, things about nondisclosure and proprietary obligations.

She was supposed to read and sign this thing. A simple exchange, that's all it was.

She'd get to stay here and find Hailey's lover—and more importantly, convince him not to be a deadbeat father. And in return, she'd share Lock's bed. Something she wanted to do anyway.

At least she *had* wanted to. Now she was wondering whether she had what it took. Like maybe she should stretch and do push-ups before putting on her pjs. And oh God, her pjs! The threadbare old camisole and shorts she'd packed would look ridiculous in this place.

Taking a fortifying breath, she read the rest of the contract. *No monies will be exchanged.* So she wasn't going to get paid for having sex with him— should she be grateful she wasn't sacrificing her morals?

Or offended she didn't warrant a tip?

She might be going mad. This was all some weird, gritty Alice in Wonderland. She'd fallen down the hole, into a land where grinning cats led her up elevators and mad hatters invited her to share a Coke. *Off with her head,* the Queen of Hearts would say, and God. God. She was so screwed.

"You haven't signed it yet," he said from behind her, his breath caressing the back of her neck, sending shivers down her spine. "Having second thoughts?"

Oh, second and third and forty-seventh thoughts. "No, I just...I always read contracts before I sign them."

"Of course you do. I bet you balance your checkbook every Sunday too."

Hah, she did not. Unless he counted the spreadsheet she updated with the downloadable statements from her bank. Which he probably would. But there was nothing wrong with that. Money management was an important life skill.

She hated money management. She hated the downloadable statements and the spreadsheets. She did them so that Chloe could go to college—except her sister had never cared that much about her classes. She did the spreadsheets so that she wouldn't end up like her mother, accepting a "date" to make rent. And most of all, she did them because she didn't know how to stop. She'd never learned how to stop being responsible and boring. She'd never learned how to live.

With shaky hands, she picked up the pen and signed her name at the bottom.

"Don't look so terrified," he said, scrawling his name beside hers. "This is going to be fun."

Exactly what she was afraid of. She had lived her life buttoned-up and tucked away. She never saw anything to long for or experienced anything to regret. It was a kind of stasis that had helped her focus on raising her sister and keeping their tiny family unit going.

Finding out about her sister's pregnancy had torn Hailey right out of her neat little box. She'd been so focused on raising Chloe that she had barely realized she was a woman now. So when was Hailey going to stop playing surrogate? Soon there would be another child to help raise, another kid who wasn't exactly hers but was still her responsibility. When was Hailey going to start living?

And once she started, once she knew how sweet it could be, how would she stop?

***

Want to read more? Three Nights with a Rock Star is available now from Amazon.com, BarnesAndNoble.com, Kobo.com, and iBooks.

Books by Shari Slade

Devil's Host MC Serial

Ride Me Hard #1

Break Me In #2

Drive Me Wild #3

Hold Me Down #4

The Half-Life Series

Three Nights with a Rock Star

One Kiss with a Rock Star

Copland College

The Opposite of Nothing

Private Study

Devil's Host MC Serial Playlist

Everybody Knows by Concrete Blonde
Slowly Freaking Out by Skylar Grey
Bones by MS MR
Send the Pain Below by Chevelle
Girls Like You by The Naked And Famous
Dead Inside by Muse
Not Your Fault by AWOLNATION
By The Throat by CHVRCHES
Take Me to Church by Hozier
Trust Fall by Incubus

Three Nights with a Rock Star Playlist

Naïve by The Kooks
Demons by Imagine Dragons
Miserable by Lit
I Hope You Suffer by AFI
The Mother We Share by CHVRCHES
Strip Me by Natasha Beddingfield
Devil In Me by Kate Voegele
Sail by AWOLNATION
Vinegar & Salt by Hooverphonic
Pour Some Sugar On Me by Emm Gryner
Can't Help Falling in Love
                    by Ingrid Michaelson
I Just Wanna Run by The Downtown Fiction
Blow It All Away by Sia
Fade Into You by Mazzy Star
Whirring by The Joy Formidable

About the Author

Shari Slade is the USA Today Bestselling and award winning author of steamy new adult, contemporary, and erotic romance. Rock stars, bikers, and bad boys. Oh my! She's a snarky optimist. A would-be academic with big dreams and very little means. When she isn't toiling away in the non-profit sector, she's writing gritty stories about identity and people who make terrible choices in the name of love (or lust). Somehow, it all works out in the end. If she had a patronus it would be a platypus.

Sign up for her newsletter at sharislade.com/newsletter to stay up-to-date on all the latest releases, happenings, and events.

Acknowledgements

A huge thank you to my bestie and number one critique partner, Skye Warren. And more huge thank yous to my awesome editors, betas, eagle-eyed proofreaders, Backstage VIPs, my author squad and my cheerleaders, especially Lea Schafer, Del Dryden, Maria Rose, Michele Harvey, Alexandra Haughton, Annika Martin, Jennifer Hanson, Julia Sykes, Molly O'Keefe, and Jenika Snow. Y'all rock.

Made in the USA
Columbia, SC
22 June 2017